THE INKLINGS
and
STAR WARS

**Rudolf Joseph Lorenz Steiner
February 27, 1861 – March 30, 1925**

THE INKLINGS
and
STAR WARS

Dr. Douglas J. Gabriel

Our Spirit, LLC
2024

OUR SPIRIT, LLC

P. O. Box 355
Northville, MI 48167

www.ourspirit.com
www.neoanthroposophy.com
www.gospelofsophia.com
www.eternalcurriculum.com

2024 Copyright © by Our Spirit, LLC

All rights reserved. No part of this publication may
Be reproduced, stored in a retrieval system, or transmitted,
in any form or by any means, electronic, mechanical,
recording, photocopying, or otherwise, without prior written
permission of the publisher.

ISBN: 978-1-963709-11-7

CONTENTS

The Inklings and Star Wars — 1
    The Influence of David Lindsay — 7
    David Lindsay — 11
    The Inkling Challenge — 13
    Who Were the Inklings? — 15
    Who Was J. R. R. Tolkien? — 16
    C. S. Lewis and Space Travel — 18
    Who was C. S. Lewis? — 21
    Charles Williams — 22
    Who Was Charles Williams? — 25
    Owen Barfield and The Inklings Challenge — 26
    Owen Barfield—the Anthroposophical Influence — 29
    Cecil Harwood, the 'Other' Anthroposophical Influence — 34
    Other Members of the Inklings — 39

The Land of Faerie — 43
    George William Russell (Æ) — 48
    Novalis (Friedrich von Hardenberg) — 53

Theosophical Thinkers with an 'Inkling' for the Spirit — 63
    Johann Wolfgang von Goethe — 65
    Friedrich von Schiller — 67
    Friedrich von Hardenberg (Novalis) — 72

Ludwig Tieck	75
Karl Wilhelm Friedrich Schlegel	79
Karl von Eckartshausen	80
Ralph Waldo Emerson—America's Spiritual Scientist	85
Source of the Force—*Star Wars* as Fairy Tale	**91**
Meeting Marcia	92
Lord of the Machines	98
A Return to Spirit	101
A Beautiful Fairy Tale	103
Conclusion	**107**
Bibliography	**111**
About Dr. Rudolf Steiner	**115**
About the Author, Dr. Douglas Gabriel	**117**
Translator's Note	**119**

The Inklings and Star Wars

We have lost the pathway to the imaginal realms from which we descended the rungs of the ladder, or steps going down the Seven Story Mountain bringing us to the emerald cube in the heart, the last vestige of the Garden of Paradise where we were once united with fiery forces of the divine creator gods. We crossed the river of forgetfulness and entered the endarkened world of the Father of Lies to witness the lonely 'other side' of creation that we collide with in the material world. As soon as the blush of youth was gone, so also was the rainbow bridge to the imaginal world where living ideas burgeon into new life continuously; a roiling sea of imaginative pictures alighting like angel wings in our minds as higher thoughts and cosmic forces wisely dancing the rhythms of creation, death, and rebirth through each moment of time.

Every shadow-image of the spirit that falls crashing into the physical world suffers the death of light—exploding and shattering into the suffering and deeds of creation's colorful plethora of diversity and beauty that is always dying and renewing life in rebirth that springs from the invisible divine world into the manifested visible world; which is an illusion, if not a delusion, enchanting newly budding consciousness. The fire of imagination is fueled by wisdom, whereas fantasies seem like delightful, effervescent, illuminous dainties that taste sweet in the mouth and bitter in the stomach and do not endure the tides of time. The Imaginal Realm is filled with spiritual beings who speak a language of unity, joining together the multiplicity of individuals. Time and space are disenchanted in the living Imaginal Realm of angelic hosts through the freely given love of human Moral Imagination, Moral Inspiration, and Moral Intuition. That is why a wise fable, fairy tale, legend, myth, or archetypal idea can dissolve space and time by existing somewhere beyond space and time, which is often indicated by the words, 'once upon a time, in a place far, far away,' and often ends with, 'and if things have not changed, they are still there today.' Fairy tales are eternal lessons concerning the divine's attempt to morally train humanity through simple Moral Imaginations that carry the message of love, beauty, truth, and goodness.

Wise imaginative tales can heal the wounds that arise from incarnating in this world of woe, this vale of tears. Finding the Holy Grail, climbing Jacob's Ladder, ascending the Seven Story Mountain, or finding enlightenment are all attainable on the first level of spirit development—Moral Imagination. If a living imaginative tale comes from a higher realm of human development, like a blessed archetype, it can serve as a healing salve of the body, an alkahest for the soul, or a spiritual balm that heals the wounds inflicted by sense perception piercing the soul with confusion, suffering, illness, old age, and death. The bridges of Moral Imagination, Moral Inspiration, and Moral Intuition can carry the soul across the abyss between the physical and spiritual worlds. Crossing to the 'other side' often necessitates feeding Cerberus, the three-headed guardian dog of Hades, and paying Charon the ferryman who transports the dead across the river Acheron. After that, the cleansed and purified 'Prince' can finally find the 'Beautiful Princess' (the soul finding the spirit), and a glorious and auspicious wedding can take place in a realm beyond the threshold between the physical and spiritual worlds. Both the bride and groom are transported from the world of mortality to the world of immortality. This magical realm is often called the Land of Faery. It is the same realm referred to in Arthurian legends as the place beneath the Stone of Bardsey Isle, where Merlin sleeps until he brings forth King Arthur from the Faery Realm of Brocéliande.

We are all called to the sacred quest to discover this new land in our dreams, visions, and inspirations of the divine, far from the impinging outer world of sense perception. It is a frightening path of self-knowledge, a hidden spiritual trace, a descent into hell, and a visit to a spiritual wedding feast within the seventh heaven which is individually created for the pure soul who treads this narrow bridge reaching into the bright lands of magic and enchantment. Truth, beauty, and goodness are the ever-present companions of the soul throughout the journey to 'one's own higher self' that should be cherished in the heart and faithfully enkindled by freely given moral impulses of love.

Some authors, in a single sentence, can take you across the threshold into another world that seems comprehensive, moral, correct, and a source of divine inspiration and beauty. Novalis (Friedrich von Hardenberg) was the master of this literary gift. In one phrase he bridges the abyss of time and space and flies into the eternal undying realms of endless births and resurrections. It is like a phrase that refreshes as if it were a drink gathered from a stream flowing forth from beneath the shrine of the Ancient of Days, a draught of thankfulness and gratitude. Novalis offers us profound wisdom in his writings, some of which he called *Pollen and Fragments*. "Only love and woman can dissolve the intellect," Novalis tells us in one of his fragments; a truth-axiom that lasts forever and unlocks long-closed doors of insight. His wisdom is a synthesis of all disciplines of knowledge distilled into a poetic equation that defines and enflames life. His words embody the 'Lost Word,' the 'Logos'—ofttimes referred to as 'the language of the birds,' 'the dragon-blood language,' 'the language of the trees,' or 'the voice of the divine'—what Christians' call 'the still small voice of God.'

Words as symbols light up like shining golden bricks in the cobbled road leading ever-onwards toward the mountain summit of our divine home. Words can become golden keys that open doors to new supersensible organs of perception, discoveries of new lands, new relationships that seem familiar and yet ancient, and the path of older memories of our personal, collective 'ancestral voice'—known in times past as ancient natural clairvoyance, or atavistic clairvoyance. The 'words' of authors and poets are keys to the etheric kingdom where *ideas* blossom into *ideals* as the reader transcends the physical and enters an ancient realm where gods shine brightly through effulgent images as large as the Cosmos and as small as a grain of sand.

J. R. R. Tolkien, the modern don of 'high fantasy' was a master at creating a living, inhabitable landscape with just one sentence, or perhaps a world with a paragraph. Tolkien shares with us where his thoughts wandered after taking up the challenge of his fellow Inklings to write fantasy stories that defy space and time. For Tolkien, that wandering included the pre-historic sinking of Atlantis, a land he called Numenor. He wrote his first story about time travel after being prompted by fellow Inklings to 'do better' than the Scottish writer David Lindsay did in his disturbing fantasy *The Voyage to Arcturus* (1920). This 'challenge' to write better novels about conquering space and time in a believable fashion led to a commitment by numerous Inklings to try their hand at writing fantasy novels that make space travel and time travel believable.

In Tolkien's first attempt to defy time and space he wrote an unfinished story entitled: *The Notion Club Papers* wherein he says:–

> "And Fire! I can't describe that. Elemental Fire: fire that is, and does not consume but is a mode or condition of physical being. But I caught sight of blazing fire, too: some real pictures. One, I think, must have been a glimpse of a meteorite hitting our air. A mountain corroded into a boulder in a few seconds of agonizing flame. But above, or between, or perhaps through all the rest, I knew endlessness. That's perhaps emotional and inaccurate. I mean Length with a capital L, applied to Time; unendurable length to mortal flesh. In that kind of dream, you can know about the feeling of aeons, of constricted waiting. Being part of the foundations of a continent, and upholding

immeasurable tons of rock for countless ages, waiting for an explosion or a world-shattering shock, is quite a common situation in parts of the universe."

All aspects of time and space travel were considered by Tolkien in the conversations found in *The Notion Club Papers*. The Notion Club was another name for the Inklings in this fantasy novel. Tolkien thoughtfully examines dreams, visions, imaginations, reincarnation, and a hundred other different considerations concerning ways to accomplish the magic-trick of 'defying' time and space. He complains that some authors are not convincing in their literary 'contrivances' they use to jump through time or leap through space. Tolkien logically complains about poor attempts that did not make him, as a reader, *willingly suspend his disbelief*.

Tolkien, in *The Notion Club Papers*, has two members of the group go 'off the deep-end' and believe they could see and feel their previous incarnations on Atlantis (Tolkien's Numenor); thus, Tolkien's 'time travel' was born. Both members of the Notion Club (probably Owen Barfield and Cecil Harwood who as anthroposophists believed in Atlantis) go somewhat mad in their insatiable desire to unravel the 'ancestral voices' sounding in their minds and the many karmic threads in their lives that bridge the present with ancient Atlantis.

Tolkien's two Notion Club members go off on a quest following 'signs' and their personal intuitions unfolding before them as they hear 'voices calling them ever further West'—Numenor/Atlantis was in the West—to the home of the immortals (the Blessed Realms) and the long-lived elves who can be found 'out beyond the Lonely Isle' (Tolerresea) on the 'Lost Road' which climbs into high heaven (Ilmen). Tolkien takes the reader up the Seven Story Mountain of spiritual ascension through time travel insinuated by the mad Notion Club members 'remembering' their previous incarnations—*a sort of reincarnational time-travel*. Tolkien describes history through the Ages of Middle-Earth and its succession of ancestors: the Elders, the long-lived Elves, the Valor, the Numenoreans, short-lived men, hobbits, and dwarfs, who are imaginatively portrayed in Tolkien's detailed histories. The entire development of humans, elves, and immortals is given in Tolkien's *Silmarillion*, published posthumously by his son Christopher Tolkien in 1977, which outlines ancient histories and indicates the future stages of ascending human consciousness.

Tolkien intended to create a history of the English people that was informed by philology, linguistics, culture, myth, legend, and imaginal history. Thus, many scholars believe 'The Inkling Challenge' was met by Tolkien in *The Lord of the Rings*, which was, of course, informed by this initial 'inkling' or 'notion' concerning ancient human history, which for Tolkien, goes back to myths of Atlantis (Numenor) and Lemuria (Tolerresea/Avallon) and even further back to Hyperborea (Valinor). While 'the Blessed Realms of Ilmen' may be the obscure realm of the Sun called Polaria; which harkens to the earliest times of creation when humans where still abiding with the heavenly gods and goddesses. Thus, Tolkien's ancient history is similar to that which Rudolf Steiner called 'Cultural Epochs': Polaria, Hyperborea, Lemuria, Atlantis, and our current cultural age called the 'Post-Atlantean Epoch.'

Tolkien takes his excursion into time travel quite seriously (*Lord of the Rings* and *Silmarillion*) but was not happy with his fantasy novel, *The Notion Club Papers* since he did not finish it nor consider it a major work for the public. One might say that Tolkien used *The Notion Club Papers* as a way to loosen up his imaginative powers to breach the 'Time Walls of the Imaginal World' and tap into a living realm of archetypes that is often called Merlin's Faery Kingdom. Tolkien has one of his main characters from *The Notion Club Papers* say:–

> "People of the future, if they only knew the records [of the Notion Club] and studied them, and let their imagination work on them, till the Notion Club became a sort of secondary world set in the Past: they could picture the real past."

The Influence of David Lindsay

There has been a long-standing story that after David Lindsay (1876-1946) wrote his book, *A Voyage to Arcturus*, in 1920; one of the Inklings brought the book to a club meeting and suggested the other members read the book and discuss it. From those discussions arose a 'challenge' to all members to write a fantasy novel that addresses the questions of time travel and space travel as Lindsay had done in his book, *A Voyage to Arcturus*. At least Tolkien, C. S. Lewis, Owen Barfield, Charles Williams, and Cecil Harwood took up the challenge quite seriously and attempted the undertaking. This pivotal moment in the history of 'high fantasy' was quite significant. Ultimately, three of the best-selling fantasy trilogies of modern times were born along with many other imaginative novels, fairy tales, and stories. As responses to The Inklings Challenge, Tolkien wrote *The Notion Club Papers* and *The Lord of the Rings*, C. S. Lewis wrote *The Dark Tower* and *The Space Trilogy*, Charles Williams wrote *Many Dimensions*, Owen Barfield wrote *The Rose on the Ash-Heap*, and Barfield's old schoolmate Cecil Harwood wrote numerous fairy tales and other stories as a Waldorf teacher.

There is some confusion about which story was written by each of these authors in response to The Inklings Challenge. A close examination of the works of these authors shows that the disagreement about which fantasy story came first is certainly debatable. Even though, a simple analysis of the storylines of these fantasies clearly reveals that even though experts debate when some of the novels were first written, it is obvious that the above-named writings clearly address time travel and space travel, whereas some of the other suggested works do not. Personally, I wanted to know which stories were written as a response because I read *A Voyage to Arcturus* after I was a big fan of Tolkien, Lewis, Barfield, Williams, and Harwood and was shocked to find that The Inklings used this strange science fiction novel to spark their efforts to write their famous fantasy novels which I loved so much.

I found David Lindsay's books, including *The Devil's Tor*, *The Violet Apple*, and *The Witch*, to be very disturbing, distressing, and completely captivating, even though he is generally considered to be an average writer in terms of skill and delivery. Lindsay is like Tolkien or Novalis in the way he quickly can create believable worlds; dramatic worlds that shake up your personal concepts and sensibilities concerning sense perception, death, philosophy, sexuality, and many other important life-questions. Lindsay writes a short description of a new place, and then suddenly, the main character has grown new sense organs to respond to the new environment. Nothing is too fantastic in Lindsay's imaginal worlds, even if it is outrageously new, original, and unheard of in the 'real world.' He even creates new colors, new sense impressions, new species, and new worlds that are believable after he takes you through portals of space travel and time travel with many gyrations and dizzying upsets to the conventional way of thinking, feeling, or perceiving. With David Lindsay's words, you quickly find yourself transported to a fascinating world where everything is shockingly new and challenging.

After reading *A Journey to Arcturus*, I gave out many copies to friends and students; but only a few were able to read it and discuss it in any sensible manner. Most were disturbed and laid it down unfinished. Some anthroposophists told me they believed it was a novel taken directly from Rudolf Steiner's *Philosophy of Freedom*; other scholars touted it as the best sci-fi novel in history. In a letter to Stanley Unwin of March 4, 1938, Tolkien says:–

> "I read *A Voyage to Arcturus* with avidity—a most comparable work, though it is both more powerful and more mythical and less rational, and also less of a story—no one could read it merely as a thriller without interest in philosophy, religion and morals."

Obviously, the book stirred something in Tolkien, as it does for most who read it all the way through and let the 'unreal become real' in their imagination. The critic, novelist, and philosopher Colin Wilson said it was the "greatest novel of the twentieth century." C. S. Lewis acknowledged it as a central influence in writing his *Space Trilogy*. Clive Barker called it "a masterpiece" and "an extraordinary work ... quite magnificent." University of Nebraska Press called it:–

> "A stunning achievement in speculative fiction. It is simultaneously an epic quest across one of the most unusual and brilliantly depicted alien worlds ever conceived, a profoundly moving journey of discovery into the metaphysical heart of the universe, and a shockingly intimate excursion into what makes us human and unique. It remains one of the most revered classics of science fiction."

Before we go further and see how this single book effected the writers of some the best-selling imaginative books in modern times, let's review the plot:

Summoned to Earth in the course of a séance, Crystalman—the evil, shape-changing deity of the solar system Arcturus—is displaced by an uninvited guest before his spirit-form can properly materialize. It is a warning. Now the mysterious guest (Maskull), his otherworldly associate, and their earthly recruit must set out for Arcturus on a strange and dangerous pilgrimage. After an interstellar journey, Maskull awakens alone in a desert on the planet Tormance, seared by the suns of the binary star Arcturus. As he journeys northward, guided by a drumbeat, he encounters a world and its inhabitants like no other, where gender is a victory won at a dear cost: where landscape and emotion are drawn into an accursed dance; where heroes are killed, reborn, and renamed; and where the cosmological lures of Shaping, who may be God, torment Maskull in his astonishing pilgrimage. At the end of his arduous and increasingly mystical quest waits a dark secret and an unforgettable revelation.

Nothing quite describes the frankness that David Lindsay uses to guide the reader into other worlds. This quality of starkness is oftentimes called 'shocking' by his critics. For instance, the interstellar trip is accomplished in a simple manner but somehow believable. The method for conveyance is a crystal spaceship that uses Arcturian 'back-rays' as the propulsion system:–

> "Maskull beheld with awe the torpedo of crystal which was to convey them through the whole breadth of visible space. It was forty feet long, eight broad, and eight high; the tank containing the Arcturian back-rays was in front, the car behind. The nose of the torpedo was directed towards the south-eastern sky. The whole machine rested upon a flat platform, raised about four feet above the level of the roof, so as to encounter no obstruction on starting its flight."
>
> "Krag flashed the light on to the door of the car, to enable them to enter. Before doing so, Maskull gazed sternly once again at the gigantic far-distant star, which was from now onwards to be their sun. He frowned, shivered slightly and got in beside Nightspore. Krag clambered past them on to his pilot's seat. He threw the torch through the open door, which was then carefully closed, fastened, and screwed up."
>
> "He pulled the starting lever. The torpedo glided gently from its platform, and passed rather slowly away from the tower, seawards. Its speed increased sensibly, though not excessively, until the approximate limits of the earth's atmosphere were reached. Krage then released the speed-valve, and the car sped on its way with a velocity more nearly approaching that of thought than of light."

Soon, Maskull sails through the Arcturus stream in his crystal spaceship to Tormance, the planet that rotates around Arcturus and its twin star. The transformation of Maskull changes his body to survive in the new and bizarre environment in a shockingly unique way:–

"He remained sprawling on the ground, as he was unable to lift his body on account of its intense weight. A numbing pain, which he could not identify with any region of his frame, acted from now onwards as a lower, sympathetic note to all his other sensations. It gnawed away at him continuously; sometimes it embittered and irritated him, at other times he forgets it."

"He felt something hard on his forehead. Putting his hand up, he discovered there a fleshy protuberance, the size of a small plum, having a cavity in the middle, of which he could not feel the bottom. Then he also became aware of a large knob on each side of his neck, an inch below the ear. From the region of his heart a tentacle had budded. It was as long as his arm, but thin, like a whipcord, and soft and flexible."

"As soon as he thoroughly realized the significance of these new organs, his heart began to pump. Whatever might, or might not, be their use, they proved one thing—that he was in a new world."

David Lindsay

Lindsay was a Scottish author best remembered for his philosophical science fiction novels. He served in the army in the First World War and was married in 1916. After the war, he moved to Cornwall with his wife to write. He said that his greatest influence was the work of George MacDonald. His novel *A Voyage to Arcturus* was published in 1920; but it was not a success, selling fewer than six hundred copies. The literary critic and author Colin Wilson has called it "the greatest imaginative work of the twentieth century," C. S. Lewis has described it as "that shattering, intolerable, and irresistible work," and Alan Moore has called it "less a novel than a private kabbalah." It also has been described as "the major underground novel of the 20th century."

Colin Wilson, the famous author of the occult, wrote an essay entitled, *The Haunted Man: Lindsay as Novelist and Mystic* that first appeared in the book *The Strange Genius of David Lindsay* (1970). The secret of Lindsay's apparent originality as a novelist, according to Wilson, lies in his metaphysical assumptions taken from Norse and other mythologies. Michael Moorcock asserted that: "Few English novels have been as eccentric or, ultimately, as influential." He noted that Alan Moore, introducing the 2002 edition, had compared the book to John Bunyan (*Pilgrim's Progress*) and Arthur Machen (*The Great God Pan*); but that it nevertheless stood "as one of the great originals." In Moorcock's view, while the book had influenced C. S. Lewis's science fiction trilogy, Lewis had "refused Lindsay's commitment to the Absolute and lacked his God-questioning genius, the very qualities which give this strange book its compelling, almost mesmerizing influence."

Lindsay's novel, *A Voyage to Arcturus* is recognized for its strangeness. Tormance's features include its alien sea, with water so dense that it can be walked upon. Gnawl water is sufficient food to sustain life on its own. The local spectrum includes two primary colors unknown on Earth, ulfire and jale, and a third color, dolm, said to be compounded of ulfire and blue. The sexuality of the Tormance species is ambiguous; Lindsay coined a new gender-neutral pronoun series, ae, aer, and aerself for the phaen who are humanoid but formed of air. Some contend that Lindsay's 'original allegory' has its own framework, which is the hierarchy of experiences on the road to enlightenment, from pleasure to pain, love, nothing, and finally something. This structure is compounded by having the protagonist examine the world in terms of the dyad of I and not-I, and the triad of 'material creation, relation, and religious feeling.' In the end, the main character (Maskull) transcends personality for dualism on both the macrocosmic and the microcosmic scales. Philosophers have speculated that the lands through which the characters travel represent philosophical systems or states of mind as Maskull searches for the meaning of life. The book combines fantasy, philosophy, and science fiction in an exploration of the nature of good and evil and their relationship with existence.

The Inkling Challenge

Christopher Tolkien tells us in the opening of the book, *The Lost Road and Other Writings*:–

> "In February 1968 my father addressed a commentary to the authors of an article about him. In the course of this he recorded that one-day C. S. Lewis said to him that since '… there is too little of what we really like in stories they would have to try to write some themselves. He went on: We agreed that he [Lewis] should try 'space-travel,' and I [Tolkien] should try 'time-travel.' His results are well known. My effort, after a few promising chapters, ran dry: it was too long a way round to what I really wanted to make, a new version of the Atlantis legend. The final scene survives as *The Downfall of Numenor*."

A few years earlier, in a letter of July 1964, J. R. R. Tolkien gave some account of his book, *The Lost Road*:–

> "When C. S. Lewis and I tossed up, and he was to write on space-travel and I on time-travel, I began an abortive book of time-travel of which the end was to be the presence of my hero in the drowning of Atlantis. This was to be called *Numenor, the Land in the West*."

In *The Fall of Numenor*, Tolkien gives us a sketchy outline of what he intended to finish as the history of Atlantis, its downfall, and its subsequent sinking beneath the waves:–

> "The Western Kingdom grows up, Atlante. Legend so named it afterward (the old name was Numar or Numenos) Atlante = The Falling. Its people [were] great mariners, and men of great skill and wisdom. They range from Toleressea to the shores of Middle-Earth. But the Gods will not allow them to land in Valinor. The Gods therefore sundered Valinor from the earth, and an awful rift appeared down which the water poured and

the armament of Atlante was drowned. They globed the whole earth so that however far a man sailed he could never again reach the West. The old line of the lands remained as a plain of air upon which only the Gods could walk, and the Eldar who faded as Men usurped the sun. But many of the Numenorie could see it or faintly see it; and tried to devise ships to sail on it. But they achieved only ships that would sail in Wilwa or lower air. Whereas the Plain of the Gods cut through and traversed Ilmen [in] which even birds cannot fly, save the eagles and hawks of Manwe."

"The gods (immortals) forbade the Elder (long-lived elves and Numenoreans) to sail beyond the Lonely Isle and would not permit any save their kings to land in Valinor. And of old, many of the Numenoreans could 'see' or 'half see' the paths to the True West and believed that at times, from a high place, they could descry the peaks of Taniquetil at the end of the Straight Road, high above the world. But upon the Straight Road only the Gods and the vanished Elves could walk, or such as the Gods summoned of the fading Elves of the round earth who became diminished in substance as Men usurped the sun. Valinor and Eressea were taken from the world into the realm of 'hidden things.' Eressea, the Lonely Isle, which is Avallon, for it is within sight of Valinor and the light of the Blessed Realm."

In *The Lost Road*, Tolkien actually speaks his heart's desire when he has his main character reflect:–

"Surveying the last thirty years, he felt he could say that his most permanent mood, thou often overlaid or suppressed, had been since childhood the desire to go back. To walk in Time, perhaps, as men walk on long roads; or to survey it, as men may see the world from a mountain, or the earth as a living map beneath an airship. But in any case, to see with eyes and to hear with ears: to see the lie of old and even forgotten lands, to behold ancient men walking, and hear their languages as they spoke them, in the days before the days, when tongues of forgotten lineage were heard in kingdoms long fallen by the shores of the Atlantic."

And then later: "I wish there was a 'Time-machine', he said aloud. "But Time is not to be conquered by machines. And I should go back, not forward; and I think backwards would be more possible."

Who Were the Inklings?

The Inklings were an informal literary discussion group associated with J. R. R. Tolkien and C. S. Lewis at the University of Oxford for nearly two decades between the early 1930s and late 1949. The Inklings were literary enthusiasts who praised the value of narrative in fiction and encouraged the writing of fantasy. The best-known, apart from Tolkien and Lewis, were Charles Williams, and Owen Barfield. As was typical for university literary groups in their time, the all-male group got together to read and discuss members' unfinished works. Early versions of Tolkien's *The Lord of the Rings*, Lewis's *Out of the Silent Planet*, and Williams's *All Hallows' Eve* were among the novels first read to the Inklings. Tolkien's fictional, unfinished novel *The Notion Club Papers* was based on the Inklings' discussion of space travel and time travel.

The name was associated originally with a society of Oxford University College, initiated by the then undergraduate Edward Tangye Lean around 1931, for the purpose of reading aloud unfinished compositions. The society consisted of students and dons, among them Tolkien and Lewis. When Edward Lean left Oxford in 1933, the society ended, and Tolkien and Lewis transferred its name to their group at Magdalen College.

Until late 1949, the Inklings' readings and discussions were usually held on Thursday evenings in C. S. Lewis's rooms at Magdalen. The

Inklings and friends were also known to gather informally on Tuesdays at midday at a local public house, The Eagle and Child. The publican, Charlie Blagrove, let Lewis and friends use his personal parlor for privacy. Later pub meetings were at the Lamb and Flag across the street, the White Horse, and the Kings Arms.

Who Was J. R. R. Tolkien?

John Ronald Reuel Tolkien (1892-1973) was an English writer, poet, philologist, and academic, best known as the author of the high-fantasy works *The Hobbit* and *The Lord of the Rings*. From 1925 to 1945, Tolkien was Professor of Anglo-Saxon at the University of Oxford. He was also a Professor of English Language and Literature which he held from 1945 until his retirement in 1959. *The Lord of the Rings* ranks as one of the most popular works of fiction of the 20th century. After Tolkien's death, his son Christopher published a series of works based on his father's extensive notes and unpublished manuscripts, including *The Silmarillion*. Tolkien's work forms a connected body of tales, poems, songs, fictional histories, invented languages, and literary essays about a fantasy world called Arda and, within it, Middle-Earth. Tolkien is identified as the 'father' of modern high-fantasy literature. Tolkien's Catholicism was a significant factor in C. S. Lewis's conversion from agnosticism to Christianity which Lewis called, 'The Great War.'

Tolkien spent more than ten years writing the primary narrative and appendices for *The Lord of the Rings*, during which time he received the constant support of the Inklings, in particular his closest friend C. S. Lewis, the author of *The Chronicles of Narnia*. Tolkien's other fantasy writings include: *Mr. Bliss, Roverandom, Tree and Leaf, The Adventures of Tom Bombadil, The Smith of Wootton Major,* and *Farmer Giles of Ham*. Most of these fantasy tales take the reader into another world by magic and enchantment; but the story that most fits The Inklings Challenge to write fantasy was Tolkien's *The Lost Road*—

an unfinished time-travel story written in late 1936 that connects Tolkien's other tales to the 20th century and is an add-on to *The Notion Club Papers*.

The Lost Road itself was also the result of the joint decision by Tolkien and Lewis to make attempts at writing science fiction concerning time travel and space travel. Lewis ended up writing a story about space travel, which eventually became his *Space Trilogy*, and Tolkien tried twice to write something about time travel, but never completed either attempt. *The Lost Road* is a fragmentary beginning of a tale, with a rough outline and several pieces of narrative, including four chapters dealing with modern England and Numenor; from which, the entire story may be glimpsed. The scheme included time travel by means of 'vision,' or being mentally inserted into what 'had been' so as to experience that which 'had happened'—a sort of reading the annals of living history. In this way, the tale links the 20th century first to the Saxon England of Alfred the Great, then to the Lombard King Albion of St. Benedict's time, the Baltic Sea during the Viking Age, Ireland at the time of the Tuatha Dé Danann's (Gaelic: 'the folk of the goddess Danu') coming (600 years after Noah's Flood), the prehistoric North in the Ice Age, a 'Galdor story' of Middle-Earth in the Third Age, and finally the Fall of Gil-galad, before recounting the prime legend of the Downfall of Numenor and the Bending of the World. The novel explores the theme of the 'Straight Road into the West,' now open only in memory because the world has become round; therein Tolkien reworked and expanded some of the ideas from *The Lost Road* and *The Notion Club Papers*.

Another wonderful Tolkien tale of magic that concerns the Land of Faery is *The Smith of Wootton Major* which takes us on a journey to the Land of Faery, thanks to the magical ingredients of the 'Great Cake of the Feast of Good Children,' a shining star that allows the person to enter Faery at any time. The Smith transcends the outer world by finding the star in the Great Cake; but it takes courage and strength to enter the Land of Faery and return to tell the tale.

The Smith had business of his own kind in Faery, and he was welcome there; for the star shone bright on his brow, and he was as safe as a mortal can be in that perilous country. The Lesser Evils avoided the 'magic star,' and from the Greater Evils he was guarded. In Faery, at first, he walked for the most part quietly among the lesser folk and the gentler creatures in the woods and meadows of fair valleys and by the bright waters in which at night strange stars shone, and at dawn the gleaming peaks of far mountains were mirrored. Some of his briefer visits he spent looking only at one tree or one flower; but later on, during longer journeys he had seen things of both beauty and terror that he could not clearly remember nor report to his friends, though he knew that they dwelt deep in his heart. But some things he did not forget, and they remained in his mind as wonders and mysteries that he often recalled.

C. S. Lewis and Space Travel

Fans of C. S. Lewis claim that *A Voyage to Arcturus* inspired Lewis to write *Out of the Silent Planet* (1938) or *Perelandra* (1943) or *That Hideous Strength* (1945), which is not necessarily true. Lewis' work, *The Dark Tower* (date of writing unknown) was not a sequel to *Out of the Silent Planet* nor *Perelandra* either. *The Dark Tower* was the original 'time and space' novel that came out of the Inklings Challenge to write a novel inspired by David Lindsay's *A Voyage to Arcturus*. This idea is evidenced in that Lewis even references the Inklings in *The Dark Tower* and their interest in time travel:–

> "With the exception of MacPhee, we might be described as a secret society: that sort of society whose secrets need no passwords, oaths, or concealment because they automatically keep themselves."

And later when he has his main character say:–

"'Well,' said Orfieu, 'time-traveling clearly means going into the future or the past. Now where will the particles that compose your body be five hundred years hence? They'll be all over the place—some in the bodies of your descendants, if you have any. Thus, to go to the year 3000 AD means going to a time at which your body doesn't exist; and that means, according to one hypothesis, becoming nothing, and, according to the other, becoming a disembodied spirit.'"

"…'The first thing I thought of, when I had abandoned the false trail of a time machine, was the possibility of mystical experience. You needn't grin MacPhee; you ought to cultivate an open mind. At any rate I had an open mind. I saw that in the writings of the mystics we had an enormous body of evidence, coming from all sorts of different times and places—and often quite independently—to show that the human mind has a power, under certain conditions, of rising to experience outside the normal time-sequence.'"

"…'To make a similar instrument for our time-perceptions we must find the time organ and then copy it. Now I claim to have isolated what I call the Z substance in the human brain. On the purely physiological side my results have been published.' MacPhee nodded."

"'But what has not yet been published,' continued Orfieu, 'is the proof that the Z substance is the organ of memory and prevision. And starting from that, I have been able to construct my chronoscope.'"

"…'On a table immediately before it stood a battery with a bulb. Higher than the bulb, and between it and the sheet, there hung a small bunch or tangle of some diaphanous material, arranged into a complicated pattern of folds and convolutions, rather reminiscent of the shapes that a mouthful of tobacco smoke assumes in the air. He gave us to understand that this was the chronoscope proper. It was only about the size of a man's fist.'"

"'I turn on the light, so,' said Orfieu, and the bulb began to shine palely in the surrounding daylight. But he switched it off again at once and continued. 'The rays pass through the chronoscope on to the reflector and our picture of the other time then appears on the sheet.'"

It seems obvious that *The Dark Tower* is Lewis's response to the challenge of conquering time and space with 'words.' It is quite significant that both Tolkien's and Lewis's first attempts were not satisfactory to the authors and therefore they didn't finish them. Tolkien's *Notion Club Papers* is an amazing story that has been pieced together by his son and has no ending. It is unresolved accept to note that Tolkien and Lewis come to a similar conclusion—space and time can be conquered by human consciousness. Tolkien met the challenge through the implications of reincarnation or simply 'remembering' the past through some mystical doorway that defies space and time. Lewis attempted the magic trick through a device that replicates what the human being can do by using their brain to transcend space and time—*the Z-substance driven chronoscope*. Lewis did not finish *The Dark Tower*, and some say he expanded it into *Perelandra* many years later. Whether this speculation is true or not, both authors have attempted to write novels that address the question of whether words can help a reader transcend space and time through a shared higher consciousness via a written story.

C. S. Lewis continued with his two fantasies (*Space Trilogy* and *The Chronicles of Narnia* series) to develop many aspects of space and time travel—whether through a 'wardrobe,' 'conscious space travel,' or 'an angel delivering a person to another planet.' Eventually, Lewis and Tolkien created some of the most beloved imaginative worlds in English literature that certainly are effective at transcending normal space and time.

In *The Dark Tower*, the oppressive atmosphere of the book is reminiscent of Lewis' own *That Hideous Strength* (1945) and David Lindsay's *A Voyage to Arcturus* (1920), which Lewis acknowledged as an influence. *The Dark Tower* does differ to a degree from the published novels of Lewis' *The Space Trilogy* in setting and subject matter. Margaret Wheatfield noted that:–

> "In *The Dark Tower* we see an alternate reality with a dark analogue of Cambridge University, where evil magic is manifest and rampant, and people are made into automatons by the sting of a magical horn."

Two quantitative stylometric analyses have compared *The Dark Tower* to other books in the Lewis space trilogy. Both analyses have supported the perception that, for whatever reason, the style of *The Dark Tower* is atypical of that employed by Lewis in the trilogy. It is often forgotten by readers that Lewis was seriously interested in science fiction long before it was fashionable. However, although Lewis was a reader of all sorts of science fiction, he himself was not interested in writing the technical side: regarding which he wrote in 1955:—

> "The most superficial appearance of plausibility—the merest sop to our critical intellect—will do. I took a hero to Mars once in a spaceship, but when I knew better, I had angels convey him to Venus."

Who was C. S. Lewis?

Clive Staples Lewis (1898-1963) was a British writer and lay theologian. He held academic positions in English literature at both Oxford University (Magdalene College, 1925-1954) and Cambridge University (Magdalene College, 1954-1963). He is best known as the author of *The Chronicles of Narnia*; but he is also noted for his other works of fiction, such as *The Screwtape Letters* and *The Space Trilogy*, and for his non-fiction Christian apologetics, including *Mere Christianity, Miracles, and The Problem of Pain*. Lewis's faith profoundly affected his work, and his wartime radio broadcasts on the subject of Christianity brought him wide acclaim.

The influences of the 'Great War' between Lewis and Tolkien that led to Lewis' conversion to Christianity deeply affected the content of Lewis' *Space Trilogy*. In the second book, *Perelandra*, there is a new Garden of Eden on the planet Venus, a new Adam and Eve, and a new 'serpent figure' to tempt Eve. The story can be seen as an account of what might have happened if the terrestrial Adam had defeated the serpent and avoided the 'Fall of Man', with the main character intervening in the novel to 'ransom' the new Adam and Eve from the deceptions of the enemy.

The Dark Tower deals with an early rendition of interdimensional travel. The story begins with a discussion of time travel among several academics at a university. They conclude that it is impossible to violate the laws of space-time in such a way. However, after the discussion, one of the men (Orfieu) unveils an invention he believes allows people to see through time. The group uses this 'chronoscope' to observe an alien world they call 'Othertime' (he does not know if it is future or past), where a group of human automatons work to construct a tower at the bidding of the story's villain. Increasingly, the observers wonder if 'Othertime' is actually the past or future, or whether it is some other reality.

Charles Williams

Another member of the Inklings who took up the challenge of trying to make the imaginal world of fantasy into a space/time travel novel was Charles Williams. Williams wrote many books, plays, and articles but he started it all off by answering 'The Inklings Challenge' to experiment with fantasy writing. Williams leaps into the deep end of the pool immediately with *Many Dimensions* by having the main character fraudulently acquire the crown of King Solomon which has a magical stone in the shape of a white and gold cube as the centerpiece. Touching or holding this magical stone gives the ability to jump from one place to another instantaneously, or to travel through time—among two of its many amazing qualities. Unfortunately, the stone reacts to the moral character of the person using it; so, when multiple copies of the stone are created and come into the possession of immoral people, all hell breaks loose, and people die. Eventually the stone is brought back into 'unity' and returned to its true owners who protect it from the evil intentions of the unworthy.

It is easy to see that *Many Dimensions* is Williams' answer to The Inklings Challenge to write a space/time travel story. Williams tells us about the origins of this magical device that defies space, time, and consciousness:–

> "'I will tell you what is said of it,' the Hajji said, 'and you shall tell Lord Arglay when he returns. It is said that in the Crown of Suleiman ben Daoud there was a strange and wonderful Stone, and it is said also that this Stone had belonged of old to the giants, to Nimrod the hunter and his children; and by its virtue Nimrod sought to build Babel which was to reach into heaven. And something of this kind is certainly possible to those who have the Stone. Before Nimrod, our Father Adam (the peace be upon him!) had it, and this only he brought with him out of Paradise when he fled before the swords of the great ones— Michael and Gabriel and Raphael (blessed be they!). And there are those who say that before then it was in the Crown of Ibliss the Accursed when he fell from heaven, and that his fall was not assured until that Stone dropped from his head. For yet again it is told that, when the Merciful One made the worlds, first of all He created that Stone and gave it to the Divine One whom the Jews call Shekinah, and as she gazed upon it the universe arose and had being.'"

Williams has not fallen into the trap that Tolkien wished to avoid by having a contrivance, a contraption that causes space and time travel to happen separate from human consciousness. William's conflation of the perfect ashlar of the Temple of Solomon and the Holy Grail—the stone from Lucifer's crown—into one little Platonic solid (cube) comprises the keystone of Solomon. This key of Solomon has long been called the 'Lost Word' of the Freemasons and is an ingenious confabulation of every sort of superpower that a device that deifies space and time should have: ancient history, cloaked in mystery, omnipotent, omnipresent, and somewhat omniscient. There was no cheap space vehicle made with tin and iron for Charles Williams. He grasped for the Holy Grail of the Hebrews and added the kabbalistic *Zohar* legends about the 'Stone of Paradise.' Consciousness as a driving force that is wed to the morality of the user is a major theme clearly explored by Williams. The consequences for manipulating immorality are merciless, like the outcome of a *Grimm's Fairy Tale*. Williams provided no mercy for the selfish user who wants to try to satiate their desires—*the usual road to hell resulting from committing the Seven Deadly Sins.*

Williams explains later in the story more details about how the Stone works and does its magic in a simple fashion:-

> "'It's the First Matter,' Sir Giles said. 'I told you that was what I thought it was, and I'm more sure than ever now. It's that which becomes everything else.' 'But how does it work?' Pallister asked. 'How does all this movement happen? How does it carry anyone about in space?'
>
> "'It doesn't,' Sir Giles answered immediately. 'Can't you see that it doesn't move people about like an airplane does. Once you are in contact, and you choose and desire and will, you go into it and come out again where you have desired because everything is in it, anyhow.'"

Who Was Charles Williams?

Charles Williams (1886-1945) was a British poet, novelist, playwright, theologian, literary critic, and member of the Inklings who met at the University of Oxford. In 1917 Williams married his first sweetheart, Florence Conway, following a long courtship during which he presented her with a sonnet sequence that would later become his first published book of poetry, *The Silver Stair*. Although Williams attracted the attention and admiration of some of the most notable writers of his day, including T. S. Eliot and W. H. Auden, his greatest admirer was probably C. S. Lewis, whose novel *That Hideous Strength* (1945) has been regarded as partially inspired by his acquaintance with Williams' novels, plays, and poems. Williams came to know Lewis after reading Lewis' then-recently published study *The Allegory of Love*; he was so impressed he jotted down a letter of congratulation and dropped it in the mail. Coincidentally, Lewis had just finished reading Williams' novel *The Place of the Lion* and had written a similar note of congratulation. The letters led to an enduring and fruitful friendship. Although chiefly remembered as a novelist, Williams also published poetry, works of literary criticism, theology, drama, history, biography, and a voluminous number of book reviews. Some of his best-known novels are *War in Heaven* (1930), *Descent into Hell* (1937), and *All Hallows' Eve* (1945). T. S. Eliot, who wrote an introduction for the last of these, described Williams' novels:—

> "...supernatural thrillers because they explore the sacramental intersection of the physical with the spiritual while also examining the ways in which power, even spiritual power, can corrupt as well as sanctify."

All of Williams' fantasies, unlike those of J. R. R. Tolkien and most of those of C. S. Lewis, are set in the contemporary world. Williams has been described by Colin Manlove as one of the three main writers of 'Christian fantasy' in the twentieth century.

Owen Barfield and The Inklings Challenge

Owen Barfield's contribution to The Inklings Challenge to write about space and time travel is suggested by some to be his first fairy tale, *The Silver Trumpet*, which has no references to either topic. In contradistinction, his unfinished novel, *The Rose on the Ash-Heap* is a mystical journey from East to West and back again until the main character, the Sultan, finally finds his long-lost love and learns to travel to the stars after winning a magic key that can open any lock—the Mater Key [Mother Key]. It seems clear that Barfield, Tolkien, and Lewis experimented with the topics and were not happy with their first product and therefore, never finished them. One witness attests to Lewis reading chapters of *The Dark Tower* many years before it was known about. It seems rather obvious that the Inklings certainly shared their first attempts at addressing transcending space and time shortly after *A Voyage to Arcturus* was published in 1920.

Barfield's *Silver Trumpet* was published in 1925, whereas *The Rose on the Ash-Heap* was from the novel, *English People*, both of which were unfinished and therefore, have no clear date associated with them. After reading other books, one can assume that *The Rose on the Ash-Heap* was Barfield's attempt at a fairy tale novel about transcending space and time and finding the Eternal Feminine.

In the Forward to *The Rose on the Ash-Heap*, Barfield says:–

> "*The Rose on the Ash-Heap* is a 'Marchen,' 26,600 words in length. Sultan, the central figure, travels daily further from the East and is eventually lost in a country not unlike the advertisement-machine and sex-ridden Eur-America which we were getting to know before the War. Formerly ruled and guided by the Lord of Albion, it is now under the total dominion of Abdol, who needs no secret police to enforce his highly centralized authority, since he uses the technique not of scarcity but of plenty."

"The story tells of Sultan's many and varied experiences, his encounters, his efforts and his lapses, until at last he finds his way out, not (like some mystics of today) by retracing his steps to the East whence he started forth, but rather by pursuing his westward journey to its utmost limit. There he finds a special master key. This he takes back with him on his final return to the West, where Abdol's blatant and horrible Fun Fair is in progress. It lets him into the secret Circus under the great ash-heap in the midst of the Fun Fair. After long and arduous training, he himself becomes a circus-rider and is united to the daughter of the Lord of Albion—the bride whom he has so long been seeking—and together with her participates in the apocalyptic end of the Fun Fair and of Abdol's reign."

Part of the 'device' for space and time travel used by Barfield's main character, the Sultan, to go anywhere in space or time was a key that fit any lock. He uses the key a great deal to open new doors of his self-discovery, even when it comes to opening the secret door to the 'underground circus,' all that is left of the palace where he finally found his true love, the temple dancer.

The Mother Key is described in the novel in the following words:–

"Now your key is a master-key. I might almost call it the master of masters. I doubt if you will find a lock anywhere that it will not open if you only have a little patience. You understand? People will be grateful. They will pay you!"

For the Sultan to prepare his heart to enter the secret circus, he first must find the last speck of hope still left in the ash-heap of the old palace to open the underground world.

Redemption comes in the story as a rose:–

"It was while his mind was full of these unquiet thoughts that Sultan observed for the first time, among the sooty weeds struggling up out of the refuse on the Heap, a garden Rose. It was a sad, spindly-looking object with one dull red knob at the top, yet there was some magic in the twilight which attracted Sultan's attention to it. It was now nearly dark, and many stars lad already appeared in the sky. Sultan looked at the flower again. Yes. It was glowing! It seemed to be giving forth a light of its own into the dusk! Or was the soft radiance that shone forth from its face no more than the diurnal gift which it had collected from the sun?"

"'I will not listen to them!' he cried determinedly. 'If I have lost the hope of happiness, I have at any rate found Peace. And that is all that the wise are able to find. The rest is illusion. "The loss of the Beloved," said the Philosopher, "is the finding of the Absolute." And have I not found the Absolute? Have I not wedded the Virgin herself? Fool! What need to travel further? I am already there!'"

Barfield eventually has the Sultan travel to the ends of the Earth in the West, where it is certain that 'no human can ever go.' There he finds a room with a domed roof open to the sky where the stars begin to speak to him of the unity between stars, although there seemingly are great spaces in between.

The ultimate space travel goal is attained:–

"In the middle of the night, Sultan was aroused by the crowing of cocks and the barking of watchdogs. Turning quickly to the East, he observed that Sirius was rising into view over the sill of the glass dome, which formed the roof of his chamber. Never had Sultan seen the Dog-Star flare and flash with such brilliancy and such violence. And as he lay there in the pleasant visionary mood betwixt sleeping and waking—that mood in which what is without seems often as if it were within, and what is within without—he gradually became aware that the furious star was singing. Sultan bent his ear attentively to the words, anxious to miss no more of them than he must have missed already, and he was only just in time; for the Song of Sirius was all but done. What he heard seemed to add to the dreamlike confusion of his mood, for at one moment it came to him as strange and new and then at another, as if he had heard it all before, a long time ago, far back in his childhood—had heard it spoke in the very same words."

"Sultan looked up, through the crown of the dome, into the zenith. No longer was the space between them empty, but as if it, too, were composed of uninterrupted star-stuff. And it was full of throbbings and workings and the throbbings and workings were themselves the violet hue of the interstellar profundity. And as he fixed his eyes on the seven great stars of the Bear, these throbbings and workings, which had drawn together at the seven points into the seven stars, seemed to him to begin boiling and seething more violently, until at last they issued from the depths above him in the form of a harmony of voices, which sang to him as if taking up all that Sirius had left unfinished: Quick! Thou shalt see the subtle bands twixt star and star—the throbbing wires, as we march singing hands in hands, in joyous companies and choirs. Sultan gazed and gazed. He thought he had never heard or seen anything so terrifying or so sweet. And then, at the end of the song of the Great Bear, followed yet another of those mysterious echoes which took Sultan back to his childhood, and with such force that he even half forgot the present and seemed to be living both parts of his life at the same moment, higher than the sphery chime!"

Owen Barfield— the Anthroposophical Influence

Arthur Owen Barfield (1898-1997) was a British philosopher, author, poet, critic, and member of the Inklings, sometimes called 'The First and Last Inkling.' He was educated at Highgate School and Wadham College, Oxford and in 1920 received a first-class degree in English language and literature. After finishing his B.Litt., which became his third book *Poetic Diction*, he was a dedicated poet and author for over ten years. After 1934 his profession was as a solicitor in London, from which he retired in 1959 aged 60. Thereafter, he had many guest appointments as Visiting Professor in North America. Barfield published numerous essays, books, and articles. His primary focus was on what he called the 'evolution of consciousness,' which is an idea which occurs frequently in his writings. He is best known as the author of *Saving the Appearances: A Study in Idolatry* and as a founding father of Anthroposophy in the English-speaking world. In 1923, he married the musician and choreographer Maud Douie. They had three adopted children, Alexander, Lucy, and Geoffrey.

Barfield had a profound influence on C. S. Lewis and, through his books *The Silver Trumpet* and *Poetic Diction* (dedicated to Lewis), an appreciable effect on J. R. R. Tolkien. Their contribution, and their conversations, persuaded both Tolkien and Lewis that myth and metaphor have always had a central place in language and literature. He once said:–

> "The Inklings work, taken as a whole, has a significance that far outweighs any measure of popularity, amounting to a revitalization of Christian intellectual and imaginative life."

Owen Barfield and C. S. Lewis met in 1919 as students at Oxford University and were close friends for 44 years. His friendship with Barfield was one of the most important in his life. Almost a year after Lewis' death, Barfield spoke of his friendship in a talk in the USA:–

> "Now, whatever he was, and as you know, he was a great many things, C. S. Lewis was for me, first and foremost, the absolutely unforgettable friend, the friend with whom I was in close touch for over 40 years, the friend you might come to

regard hardly as another human being, but almost as a part of the furniture of my existence."

When they met, Lewis was an atheist/agnostic who told Barfield, "I don't accept God!" Barfield was influential in converting Lewis. Lewis came to see that there were two kinds of friends, a first friend with whom you feel at home and agree and a second friend who brings to you a different point of view. He found Barfield's contribution in this way particularly helpful despite, or because of, the fact that "during the 1920s, the two were to engage in a long dispute over Barfield's (and their mutual friend, A. C. Harwood's) connection to Anthroposophy and the kind of knowledge that imagination can give us…"—which they affectionately called 'The Great War.' Through their conversations, Lewis gave up materialistic realism—the idea that our sensible world is self-explanatory and is all that there is—and moved closer to what he had always disparagingly referred to as 'super-naturalism' or Christianity. These conversations influenced Lewis towards writing his *Chronicles of Narnia* series. As well as being friend and teacher to Lewis, Barfield was (professionally) his legal adviser and trustee.

Barfield was an important intellectual influence on Lewis. Lewis wrote his 1949 book *The Lion, the Witch and the Wardrobe*, the first *Narnia Chronicle*, for his friend's adopted daughter Lucy Barfield and dedicated it to her. He also dedicated *The Voyage of the Dawn Treader* to Barfield's son Geoffrey in 1952.

Barfield also influenced Lewis' scholarship and worldview. He dedicated his first scholarly book, *The Allegory of Love* (1936) to his "wisest and best of my unofficial teachers," stating in its preface that he asked no more than to disseminate Barfield's literary theory and practice. Barfield's 'more than merely intellectual' approach to philosophy is illustrated by a well-known interchange that took place between himself and Lewis, which Lewis did not forget. Lewis one day made the mistake of referring to philosophy as 'a subject.' "It wasn't a subject to Plato," said Barfield, "it was a way." In the third lecture of *The Abolition of Man* (1947), Lewis suggests that Barfield's mentor, Rudolf Steiner [founder of Anthroposophy, or Spiritual Science], may have found the way to a "redeemed scientific method that does not omit the qualities of the observed object."

It is to be expected that writers will have a muse, and it seems that Lucy Barfield was that muse for C. S. Lewis. Lewis wrote the following dedication in his novel, *The Lion, the Witch and the Wardrobe* to his goddaughter, Lucy Barfield:–

> "My Dear Lucy, I wrote this story for you, but when I began it, I had not realized that girls grow quicker than books. As a result, you are already too old for fairy tales, and by the time it is printed and bound you will be older still. But someday you will be old enough to start reading fairy tales again. You can then take it down from some upper shelf, dust it, and tell me what you think of it. I shall probably be too deaf to hear, and too old to understand a word you say, but I shall still be your affectionate godfather."

Lucy was an accomplished dancer, musician, composer, artist, and poet. She had a special vitality which inspired both her father and godfather (Barfield and Lewis respectively). The character of Lucy Pevensie appears to be based in part on Lucy herself, sharing her name, fair hair, and lively personality. In spite (or perhaps because) of her debilitating condition, Lucy served as a muse and inspiration to her father, Owen Barfield, representing the Eternal-Feminine in his myth allegory, *The Rose on the Ash-Heap*.

Barfield was also an important influence on Tolkien. Lewis wrote to Barfield in 1928 about his influence on Tolkien:–

> "You might like to know that when Tolkien dined with me the other night he said, apropos of something quite different,

that your conception of the ancient semantic unity had modified his whole outlook, and he was always just going to say something in a lecture when your concept stopped him in time."

Barfield became an Anthroposophist after attending a lecture by Rudolf Steiner in 1924. He studied the work and philosophy of Rudolf Steiner throughout his life, translated some of his works, and had some of his own early essays published in Anthroposophical publications. This part of Barfield's literary work includes the book *The Case for Anthroposophy*, containing his *Introduction* to selected extracts from Steiner's *Riddles of the Soul*. Steiner was always a formative presence in Barfield's work, probably his major influence; but Barfield's thought should not be considered merely derivative of Steiner's. Barfield considered Steiner a much greater man in possession of a greater mind than Goethe.

Barfield might be characterized as both a Christian writer and a learned anti-reductionist writer. His books include: *Unancestral Voice; History, Guilt, and Habit; Romanticism Comes of Age; The Rediscovery of Meaning; Saving the Appearances; Speaker's Meaning; Worlds Apart; and History in English Words,* among others. Barfield was also an influence on T. S. Eliot who called Barfield's book *Worlds Apart,* "a journey into seas of thought very far from ordinary routes of intellectual shipping."

In a foreword to *Poetic Diction*, Howard Nemerov, U.S. Poet Laureate, stated:–

> "Among the poets and teachers of my acquaintance who know *Poetic Diction* it has been valued not only as a secret book, but nearly as a sacred one."

Saul Bellow, the Nobel Prize winning novelist, wrote:–

> "We are well supplied with interesting writers, but Owen Barfield is not content to be merely interesting. His ambition is to set us free. Free from what? From the prison we have made

for ourselves by our ways of knowing, our limited and false habits of thought, our common sense."

The culture critic and psychologist James Hillman called Barfield "one of the most neglected important thinkers of the 20th Century." Barfield likely believed that fairy tales were educationally valuable because as an active anthroposophist emphasizing human consciousness and language, he agreed with Rudolf Steiner's views that included the importance of fairy tales for child development, which were taught in Steiner's Waldorf schools. For instance, Barfield's story *The Child and the Giant* was written for his Upper School English class at The New School, Streatham in 1930, a Waldorf school.

Cecil Harwood, the 'Other' Anthroposophical Influence

Alfred Cecil Harwood (1898-1975) was a lecturer, Waldorf teacher, writer, editor, Anthroposophist and an often unacknowledged member of the Inklings. Cecil Harwood attended school together with Owen Barfield, who became his life-long friend and co-worker in many areas of his life. Together they studied at Oxford University and were part of the circle of the Inklings that included C. S. Lewis and J. R. R. Tolkien. His friendship with Daphne Olivier, who later became his wife, led him to meet Rudolf Steiner and subsequently to found the first Waldorf school in England, the so-called 'New School' that later became Michael Hall, together with her and three other colleagues. He remained connected to the school for the rest of his life.

Daphne and Cecil had five children and worked together for over 25 years. In 1948, a Swedish/English eurythmist by the name of Marguerite Lundgren had begun working in England and was dedicated to English-language eurythmy and had become friends with both Owen Barfield and the Harwoods. She and Harwood married in 1953, beginning another fruitful co-working as they built up the eurythmy work in England with performances, international tours, the London School of Eurythmy, and finally the book on which they collaborated with Marjorie Raffe, *Eurythmy and the Impulse of Dance*.

Cecil Harwood had joined the Anthroposophical Society in Great Britain shortly after meeting Rudolf Steiner for the first time in 1924. In 1937, he became its chairman and General Secretary, a position he carried until 1974. In this capacity, he was instrumental not just in developing the work in the United Kingdom but also in re-establishing the international relationships within the Anthroposophical Society, as a whole, after the internal difficulties of the 1930s and 1940s. This implied a certain amount of travel which he undertook not just on behalf of the Society but also in assisting the growth and development of Waldorf education worldwide, and in particular, in the United States. He was founder and for many years editor of *Child and Man*, the journal of the Waldorf Steiner schools in Great Britain, as well as writing one of the definitive works on Waldorf Education for the English-speaking world: *The Recovery of Man in Childhood*.

Harwood's friendship with Owen Barfield and C. S. Lewis has been well-recorded in the biographies written on these two personalities. It seems to have been a fruitful relationship throughout, influencing the work and thought of all three. As C. S. Lewis said in *Surprised by Joy*, "Cecil Harwood is the sole Horatio known to me in this age of Hamlets."

In 1922 at the age of twenty-four, Alfred Cecil Harwood, with his lifelong friend Owen Barfield, attended an English folksong and dance festival in Cornwall. It was there that Harwood and Barfield would encounter the work of Rudolf Steiner by meeting Daphne Olivier.

Cecil Harwood began his career with the hope of becoming a writer. He had neither the intention nor the ambition to become a teacher or head of a national organization, yet he became an exemplary teacher, a well-respected leader, and a celebrated author, editor, translator, and lecturer.

Cecil Harwood's son, Laurence Harwood was one of the few remaining people who really knew C. S. Lewis (Jack). In Laurence's book, *C.S. Lewis, My Godfather: Letters, Photos, and Recollections,* he talks about the relationships Lewis had with his father, Owen Barfield, and Laurence's mother, Daphne. The book provides us with a picture of Lewis as a family man, enjoying treks with his friends, delighting in the visits with the Harwood children, and letters that have an intellectual wit that opens doors into the lives of them all.

Laurence said that he and Lewis exchanged letters at all stages of his life, from childhood to adolescence to adulthood, and until Lewis' death in 1963, far more than is typical of a godfather. He said that Lewis adapted his writing to every level and often drew pictures in the margins. Laurence kept every letter and shares them in his book.

When Laurence experienced 'failure' at Oxford due to his lack of being a natural academic, and double pneumonia, while taking preliminary examinations, Lewis not only encouraged Laurence to pursue a different vocation but paid for him to attend the Royal Agricultural College to undergo training to become a land agent and surveyor. Lewis followed up by paying for Laurence's education.

For C. S. Lewis, the walks that he took each Eastertide with Owen Barfield, Walter O. Field, and Cecil Harwood epitomized friendship. Although they were distinctly different in personality and were not all interested in the same things, the four 'cretaceous perambulators' shared core ideals and aspirations. Their writings are evidence of the wonderful strengths of their friendship. For many years, walking tours with friends and with his brother were a highlight of his vacations, as his letters attest. Lewis began the practice in the mid-1920s when two of his friends, Owen Barfield and Cecil Harwood invited him to join them on a walk during a vacation between terms at Oxford University where the three of them were then students. Each year thereafter, until the Second World War made such excursions impossible, Lewis, Barfield, and Harwood, often together with one or two others, took an Eastertide walking holiday.

The four had many interests and tastes in common. Harwood's son Laurence notes:–

"A shared love of classics, myths and legends, philosophy and ancient history, Greek and Latin, English literature, opera and walking tours cemented the camaraderie of the three undergraduate friends [Barfield, Harwood and Lewis] during their time at Oxford and for the rest of their lives."

For a time, Field and Barfield enthusiastically advocated the Social Credit Movement which began in the early 1920s, inspired by the ideas of C. H. Douglas. In 1923, however, they and Harwood began to investigate the ideas of the Austrian philosopher and reformer, Rudolf Steiner, who had been the featured speaker in a Conference on *Spiritual Values in Education and Social Life* held at Oxford's Manchester College in the summer of 1922. One of those who were lastingly inspired by what Steiner said in Oxford was Daphne Olivier (later Daphne Harwood), whom Harwood and Barfield had met in the Falmouth Music Club. It was through her that Harwood, Barfield, Field, and Lewis first learned about Anthroposophy, the 'science of the spirit' inaugurated by Steiner and found that in Steiner's conception of the "Threefold Commonwealth," with its harmony of the economic, political, and spiritual spheres, their dreams for a balanced social life found a home.

For their part, Harwood, Barfield, and Field did not rush to embrace Anthroposophy. For several months they read and discussed Steiner's writings and carefully examined his ideas by testing them against what they already knew and holding them up to Lewis' critical scrutiny. Gradually, their initial skepticism was replaced by confidence that Anthroposophy emphasized clear, wide-awake, independent thinking, and thus could rightfully appeal to all who felt themselves "spirits in bondage."

As Barfield wrote in his first published statement about Anthroposophy:–

"...anybody who feels an instinctive distrust of authority and dogma, whether it emanates from a Church, a Mahatma Letter, or a science lecture-room, and who at the same time believes that knowledge has a somewhat more inviting future before it than the prospect of tracing the law of cause and effect one step further back behind the electron, is making a great mistake if he does not put himself to the trouble of finding out whether Steiner has anything to tell him."

Harwood, Field, and Barfield were especially impressed by the practicality and constructiveness of Steiner's ideas, which opened promising new ways of working in a variety of other fields, including not only economics but also education, the arts, agriculture, and medicine. Together with three others, Cecil and Daphne Harwood founded the first Steiner School in the English-speaking world.

The Christ-centeredness of Rudolf Steiner's outlook also was decisively important for Harwood, Field, and Barfield. Like Lewis, they were deeply religious men. Both Harwood and Field were strongly connected with The Christian Community, a worldwide movement for religious renewal which was founded soon after the Great War with the help of Rudolf Steiner.

In 1926, Lewis abandoned philosophical realism and became an absolute idealist; and in 1929 he exchanged idealism for theism:–

"I gave in and admitted that God was God, and knelt and prayed, perhaps the most dejected and reluctant convert in all of England."

Also in 1929, Barfield wrote his second novel, *English People*. It provides an interesting perspective on the 'walking together' of Lewis, Field, Barfield, and Harwood, for, like the four real-life friends, each of the four central characters has a distinctly different outlook from the others, and much of the novel consists of conversations in which they examine their shared ideas and ideals from the multiple points of view represented in their circle of friends.

Lewis quietly died at the Kilns, his home. Among the small group of family and friends who attended his funeral were Barfield and Harwood. Lewis had named these two the executors of his will and trustees of his estate.

Other Members of the Inklings

Warren Hamilton Lewis, C. S. Lewis's brother (1895-1973) was a British historian and officer in the British Army, best known as the elder brother of the author and professor C. S. Lewis. Warren Lewis was a supply officer with the Royal Army Service Corps of the British Army during and after the First World War. After retiring in 1932 to live with his brother in Oxford, he was one of the founding members of the Inklings. He wrote on French history and served as his brother's secretary for the later years of C. S. Lewis's life.

Christopher John Reuel Tolkien, J. R. R. Tolkien's son, (1924-2020) was an English academic editor, becoming a French citizen in later life. He was the son of author J. R. R. Tolkien and the editor of much of his father's posthumously published work. Tolkien drew the original maps for his father's *The Lord of the Rings*. Tolkien had long been part of the critical audience for his father's fiction, first as a child listening to tales of Bilbo Baggins (which were published as *The Hobbit*), and then as a teenager and young adult offering much feedback on *The Lord of the Rings* during its 15-year gestation. He had the task of interpreting his father's sometimes self-contradictory maps of Middle-Earth in order to produce the versions used in the books, and he re-drew the main map in the late 1970s to clarify the lettering and correct some errors and omissions. Tolkien was invited by his father to join the Inklings when he was 21 years old, making him the youngest member of the informal literary discussion society. Christopher Tolkien published *The Saga of King Heidrek the Wise*, translated from the Icelandic with introduction, notes, and appendices in 1960. Later, Tolkien followed in his father's footsteps, becoming a lecturer and tutor in English Language at New College, Oxford, from 1964 to 1975. In 2016, he was given the Bodley Medal, an award that recognizes outstanding contributions to literature, culture, science, and communication.

Roger Lancelyn Green (1918-1987) was a part-time professional actor from 1942 to 1945, deputy librarian of Merton College, Oxford, from 1945 to 1950 and William Nobel Research Fellow in English Literature at the University of Liverpool from 1950 to 1952. He became known primarily for his writings for children, particularly his retellings of the myths of Greece (*Tales of the Greek Heroes and The Tale of Troy*) and Egypt (*Tales of Ancient Egypt*), as well the Norse mythology (*The Saga of Asgard,* later renamed *Myths of the Norsemen*) and the stories of King Arthur (*King Arthur and His Knights of the Round Table*) and Robin Hood (*The Adventures of Robin Hood*). His works of original fiction include *The Luck of Troy*, set during the Trojan War, and *The Land of the Lord High Tiger*, a fantasy that has been compared to the *Narnia* books.

He studied under C. S. Lewis at Merton College, Oxford, where he obtained a B.Litt. degree. As an undergraduate, he performed in the Oxford University Dramatic Society's Shakespeare dramas produced by Nevill Coghill. He was deputy librarian at Merton College from 1945 to 1950, then William Noble Research Fellow in English Literature at the University of Liverpool from 1950 to 1952. As Andrew Lang Lecturer at the University of St. Andrews from 1968 to 1969, he delivered the 1968 Andrew Lang lecture.

Lancelyn Green remained close to Lewis until the latter's death in 1963 and holidayed in Greece with Lewis and his wife Joy Gresham just before her death from cancer in 1960. When Lewis started writing the Narnia books in the late 1940s, Lancelyn Green suggested that they should be called *The Chronicles of Narnia.* Lancelyn Green lived in Cheshire at Poulton Hall, a manor house that his ancestors had owned for more than 900 years; he was Lord of the Manors of Poulton-Lancelyn and Lower Bebington.

Lord Edward Christian David Gascoyne-Cecil (1902-1986) was a British biographer, historian, and scholar. He held the style of 'Lord' by courtesy, as a younger son of a marquess. In 1939, he became a Fellow of New College, Oxford, where he remained a Fellow until 1969, when he became an Honorary Fellow. In 1947, he became Professor of Rhetoric at Gresham College, London, for a year; but in 1948 he returned to the University of Oxford and remained a Professor of English Literature there until 1970.

Henry Victor Dyson (1896-1975), generally known as Hugo Dyson and who signed his writings H. V. D. Dyson, was an English academic and a member of the Inklings literary group. He was a committed Christian, and together with J. R. R. Tolkien he helped C. S. Lewis to convert to Christianity, particularly after a long conversation as they strolled on Addison's Walk at Oxford. Dyson preferred talking at Inklings meetings rather than reading. He had a distaste for J. R. R. Tolkien's *The Lord of the Rings* and complained loudly at its readings. Eventually Tolkien gave up reading to the group altogether.

Dr. Robert Emlyn Havard (1901-1985) was the physician of C. S. Lewis, his wife Joy Gresham, and J. R. R. Tolkien. Havard has also been credited as a "skilled and prolific writer." In addition to his medical research papers, Havard authored an appendix for C. S. Lewis' *The Problem of Pain* as well as a description of Lewis included in *Remembering C. S. Lewis: Recollections of Those Who Knew Him*, and one of J. R. R. Tolkien included in *Mythlore*.

Lewis invited Havard to join the Oxford-based Inklings because of the literary interests he shared with the group. Like Tolkien, he was a Roman Catholic. Havard was sometimes referred to by the Inklings as the "Useless Quack," mainly because Warren Lewis once called him so upon being irritated by his tardiness, and his brother, Jack (C. S.), thought it quite amusing at the time and caused the nickname to continue. The abbreviation "U.Q." was thereafter a common reference to Havard.

Adam Fox (1883-1977), Canon, was the Dean of Divinity at Magdalene College, Oxford. He was one of the first members of the literary group. He was Oxford Professor of Poetry and later he became Canon of Westminster Abbey. He was also warden of Radley College. He was headmaster of the Radley College (1918-1924). Between 1938 and 1942 he was Oxford Professor of Poetry. He is buried in Westminster Abbey in Poets' Corner.

During his time at Oxford, he wrote his long poem in four books *Old King Coel*. It gets its name from King Cole, legendary British father of the Roman Empress Helena, the mother of the Emperor Constantine. As Professor of Poetry, Fox advocated for poetry which is intelligible to readers, and gives enough pleasure to be read again.

Nevill Henry Kendal Aylmer Coghill (1899-1980) was an Anglo-Irish literary scholar, known especially for his modern English version of Geoffrey Chaucer's *Canterbury Tales*.

The Land of Faerie

Undoubtedly, members of the Inklings were enamored with the mystical and mythic Land of Faerie. Numerous members of the group attempted to help their readers travel into this magic imaginal kingdom where the deep secrets and truths of life are found. The long tradition of fairy tales was part of the foundation to which the Inklings added high-fantasy with its brilliant poetic visions of ancient history and their maps of the roads to higher worlds found across the 'bridge of imagination' that defies space and time. These great writers wished to go much further than just speculation, they strove to find 'moral' imaginations that emanate from the realms of beings not bound by human limitations. Like the Norse Aesir god Heimdall, the watchman of the rainbow bridge called Bifrost, they had extraordinary capacities to see and hear all that goes on in the upper realms of the Land of Faerie and share that wisdom with those below longing to rise to the castles of the gods. The Inklings were guardians of the imaginal realm that Rudolf Steiner and Anthroposophists call Moral Imagination. These realms exist separately above the human world and were home to the gods of Asgard, what we might call angels of imagination. Heimdall allowed the upper gods to cross Bifrost from Asgard to the human's domain when they were on a mission to help aid and inspire humanity. Vanir gods, frost giants, and humans were not allowed to cross the rainbow bridge into the imaginal world until they had gained the favor of the upper gods. This is much akin to the power of high-fantasy to awaken imaginal capacities to behold far and wide the workings of the gods in all realms.

The inspired Inklings spent their lives trying to reveal moral messages from the gods to the anxiously seeking humans who intuit that there is something more to life than a banal existence plowing the fields of suffering to gain immortal life; or at least, to find a semblance of something greater than this earthly vale of tears. The developed human 'moral imagination' gives the soul the capacity to walk across the rainbow bridge into the fairyland of the spirit. This is where the higher virtues and ancient wisdom lore of the gods still exist in a refined and beautiful world filled with heavenly light, truth, and goodness. All that gives life to the earth burgeons forth from this wellspring of inspiration that enkindles the fiery love found in the heart of a truth seeker. The Inklings interacted with this immortal realm of the gods in many of their stories and attempted to offer wings to the imagination of humans who wish to fly where no earthly human may go without first surrendering the gravity of life that carries the earthly weight that the rainbow bridge cannot endure. Pain and suffering are healed in the Land of Faerie through hearing the tales that free the soul to soar like eagles into the divine realms of the upper worlds.

J. R. R. Tolkien was akin to the realm of faerie and drew forth more celestial images of the upper worlds than most any other high-fantasy author. Tolkien was like Heimdall, listening for the sounds of harmony and dissonance from both the upper and lower worlds and maintaining his faithful guardianship of morality and virtue that connect the earth to heaven. He stood guard at the passageway to higher imagination that unites the glory and splendor of the past with the bright hope of the future. It is quite instructive to hear what Tolkien has to say about the Land of Faerie as a guide to the realms in which he so often dwelt.

The following quotations are taken from, *On Fairy Stories*, by J. R. R. Tolkien:–

> "Faerie is a perilous land, and in it are pitfalls for the unwary and dungeons for the overbold…"

> "Faerie cannot be caught in a net of words; for it is one of its qualities to be indescribable, though not imperceptible."

"Behind the fantasy, real wills and powers exist, independent of the minds and purposes of men."

"But since the fairy-story deals with 'marvels,' it cannot tolerate any frame or machinery suggesting that the whole story in which they occur is a figment or illusion."

"It is plain enough that fairy-stories (in wider or in a narrower sense) are very ancient indeed. Related things appear in very early records; and they are found universally, wherever there is language."

"The history of fairy-stories is probably more complex than the physical history of the human race, and as complex as the history of human language. All three things: independent invention, inheritance, and diffusion, have evidently played their part in producing the intricate web of Story."

"The land of fairy-story is wide and deep and high and is filled with many things: all manner of beasts and birds are found there; shoreless seas and stars uncounted; beauty that is an enchantment, and an ever-present peril; both sorrow and joy as sharp as swords. In that land a man may (perhaps) count himself fortunate to have wandered, but its very riches and strangeness make dumb the traveler who would report it. And while he is there it is dangerous for him to ask too many questions, lest the gates shut, and the keys be lost. The fairy gold too often turns to withered leaves when it is brought away. All I can ask is that you, knowing these things, will receive my withered leaves, as a token that my hand at least once held a little of the gold."

"This enchantment of distance, especially of distant time, is weakened only by the preposterous and incredible Time Machine itself. But we see in this example one of the main reasons why the borders of fairy-story are inevitably dubious. The magic of Faerie is not an end in itself, its virtue is in its operations: among these are the satisfaction of certain primordial human desires. One of these desires is to survey the depths of space and time. Another is (as will be seen) to hold communion with other living things. A story may thus deal with the satisfaction of these desires, with or without the operation of either machine or magic, and in proportion as it succeeds it will approach the quality and have the flavor of a fairy-story. Next, after travelers' tales, I would also exclude, or rule out of order, any story that uses the machinery of Dream, the dreaming of actual human sleep, to explain the apparent occurrence of its marvels."

"It is true that Dream is not unconnected with Faerie. In dreams strange powers of the mind may be unlocked. In some of them a man may for a space wield the power of Faerie, that power which, even as it conceives the story, causes it to take living form and color before the eyes. A real dream may indeed sometimes be a fairy-story of almost elvish ease and skill—while it is being dreamed. But if a waking writer tells you that his tale is only a thing imagined in his sleep, he cheats deliberately the primal desire at the heart of Faerie: the realization, independent of the conceiving mind, of imagined wonder."

"Even fairy-stories, as a whole, have three faces: the Mystical towards the Supernatural; the Magical towards Nature; and the Mirror of scorn and pity towards Man. The essential face of Faerie is the middle one, the Magical. But the degree in which the others appear (if at all) is variable and may be decided by the individual storyteller."

"What really happens is that the story-maker proves a successful 'sub-creator.' He makes a Secondary World which your mind can enter. Inside it, what he relates is 'true': it accords with the laws of that world. You therefore believe it, while you are, as it were, inside."

"To make a Secondary World inside which the green sun will be credible, commanding Secondary Belief, will probably require labor and thought, and will certainly demand a special skill, a kind of elvish craft. Few attempt such difficult tasks. But when they are attempted, and in any degree accomplished, then we have a rare achievement of Art: indeed narrative art, story-making in its primary and most potent mode."

"Enchantment produces a Secondary World into which both designer and spectator can enter, to the satisfaction of their senses while they are inside; but in its purity it is artistic in desire and purpose."

"To the elvish craft, Enchantment and Fantasy aspires, and when it is successful all forms of human art most nearly approach. Fantasy is a natural human activity. It certainly does not destroy or even insult Reason; and it does not either blunt the appetite for, nor obscure the perception of, scientific verity."

"Fantasy remains a human right: we make in our measure and in our derivative mode, because we are made and not only made, but made in the image and likeness of a Maker. It is easy for the student to feel that with all his labor he is collecting only a few leaves, many of them now torn or decayed, from the countless foliage of the Tree of Tales, with which the Forest of Days is carpeted. It seems vain to add to the litter. Who can design a new leaf?"

"Creative fantasy, because it is mainly trying to do something else (make something new), may open your hoard and let all the locked things fly away like cagebirds. The gems all turn into flowers or flames, and you will be warned that all you had (or knew) was dangerous and potent, not really effectively chained, free and wild; no more yours than they were you."

"It was in fairy-stories that I first divined the potency of the words, and the wonder of the things, such as stone, and wood, and iron; tree and grass; house and fire; bread and wine. The peculiar quality of the 'joy' in successful Fantasy can thus be as a sudden glimpse of the underlying reality or truth. It is not only a 'consolation' for the sorrow of this world, but a satisfaction, and an answer to that question: Is it true?"

"The *Gospels* contain a fairy-story, or a story of a larger kind which embraces all the essence of fairy-stories. They contain many marvels—peculiarly artistic, beautiful, and moving: 'mythical' in their perfect, self-contained significance; and among the marvels is the greatest and most complete conceivable Eucatastrophe—a happy ending."

"The Christian joy, the Gloria, is of the same kind; but it is preeminently (infinitely, if our capacity were not finite) high and joyous. But this story is supreme; and it is true. Art has been verified. God is the Lord of angels and of men—and of elves. Legend and History have met and fused."

George William Russell (Æ)

There are numerous authors who courted the Land of Faerie and Æ (George Russell) was one of the best who captured the enchantment of higher worlds and brought it home as poetry and fairy- stories that elevate the soul to the realms of virtuous enrichment. Just as the Inklings were familiar with Rudolf Steiner's Anthroposophy, Æ was a deep student of the mystical and philosophical thinkers associated with the Theosophical Society of H. P. Blavatsky. Great masters of wisdom were rumored to have inspired Blavatsky and many other theosophically inspired writers, of which Æ was a prominent example. His poetry, stories, and paintings transport the soul into higher worlds where morality and virtue reign supreme. He too, like the Inklings, hoped that the imaginal realms would provide the spirit nourishment so desperately needed in the dark world of human suffering. Reading Æ is equivalent to donning the wings of spirit and mounting the skies of moral imagination and inspiration that are eternal and unblemished by darkness and ignorance. A true healing of the soul can be the result of reading one of his stories, which awakens the higher nature of the reader to the comforting truths of wisdom. Æ was not an Inkling, but certainly his inspiration arose from the same well-springs of the upper gods of the imaginal world where divine beings beckon the truth seeker to rise to their new home in the Land of Faerie, the spirit world of morality and love.

George William Russell was an Irish poet, painter, essayist, and mystic who wrote under the pseudonym "A. E." (Æ); a name he chose to align with the theosophical concept of the Æon. Born April 10, 1867, in Northern Ireland, his family moved to Dublin when he was ten. He had a natural talent for painting and attended the Metropolitan School of Art in Dublin, where he met William Butler Yeats who introduced him to Theosophy. At that time, Russell earned his living by working as a clerk and soon began contributing poems and articles to *The Irish Theosophist*.

Yeats was influenced by Russell's wide knowledge of esoteric philosophies and Irish mythology; Æ's *The Candle of Vision* (1918) is the fullest exposition of those mystical beliefs. His first collection of verse, *Homeward: Songs by the Way* (1894) contained numerous fusions of Theosophy and Irish mythology. His subsequent collections include *The Earth Breath* (1897), *The Divine Vision* (1904), *Voices of the Stones* (1925), and *Midsummer Eve* (1928). His *Collected Poems* appeared in 1913. While much of his verse is of a rather visionary character, occasional pieces form simple adaptations of folk themes. *The Candle of Vision* (1918), a collection of essays describing his inner life, is a poetic rendering of high spiritual truth and philosophy. His two novels, *The Interpreters* (1922) and *The Avatars* (1933) outline his spiritual message and point at the bridge connecting earth to heaven.

In 1922, Russell became editor of *The Irish Statesman*, which incorporated *The Irish Homestead*, and he continued in that role until 1930. He continued writing poems and prose, publishing collections such as *Enchantment and Other Poems* (1930) and *The House of the Titans and Other Poems* (1934). The prose work *Song and Its Fountains* (1932), continues the spiritual and philosophical enquiry begun in *The Candle of Vision*. He went to live in England after 1933, first in London and then in Bournemouth. Throughout all his work, Æ stayed true to his quest to enter the Land of Faerie and return home with the magic gold of wisdom and insight.

> From: *Shadow and Substance,* by Æ
> "For we miss to hear the fairy tale of time, the aeonian chant radiant with light and color which the spirit prolongs. The warnings are not for those who stay at home, but for those who adventure abroad. They constitute an invitation to enter the mysteries."

In *The Avatars* (1933), Æ created a 'futurist fantasy' in which mythical heroes, or avatars, appear and spread joy wherever they go. They are removed by the authorities, but their cult grows through legends and artistic renderings until they disappear from the earth and enter the enchanted land of spirit.

> From: *The Avatars,* by Æ
> "I thought it beautiful. In it [the play] the soul was led by music to the fairy world. There were songs by invisible singers hidden behind rocks or trees on the hills. Song and

music became more ethereal as they came from the heights. But the real wonder came when the voices had died upon the hills, for there then sounded a melody played on a violin, a music not born out of any human emotion, but the melody of aether itself, a tapestry of sound wavering between earth and heaven. I felt if that magical curtain lifted, I would be in Paradise. When it died inaudible by the ear it was still audible by the spirit."

"…The universe itself was nothing but Imagination ceaselessly creative. The Imagination and Will which uphold it are in us also, so that we can make our own world and transfigure it out of the glory still within us. We were not what we seemed, but children of the heavens. The body even is a palace all marvelous within. It has secret radiant gateways opening inward to light. It has wings which could be unfolded. All the precious fires of Elohim are co-mingled in us. She said there were many who came in the past from that heaven world of light, divine poets, who made known the path between earth and heaven. This they did less by speech than by opening the blind eyes and showing images of gods and immortals in a clear, immovable and blessed light."

From: *The Slave of the Lamp*, by Æ
"I found every intense imagination, every new adventure of the intellect endowed with magnetic power to attract to it its own kin. Will and desire were as the enchanter's wand of fable, and they drew to themselves their own affinities."

From: *The Many-Colored Land*, by Æ
"I know that my brain is a court where many living creatures throng, and I am never alone in it. You, too, can know that if you heighten the imagination and intensify the will. The darkness in you will begin to glow, and you will see clearly,

and you will know that what you thought was but a mosaic of memories is rather the froth of a gigantic ocean of life, breaking on the shores of matter, casting up its own flotsam to mingle with the life of the shores it breaks on. If you will light your lamp, you can gaze far over that ocean and even embark on it."

"When thought or imagination is present in me, ideas or images appear on the surface of consciousness, and though I call them my thoughts, my imaginations, they are already formed when I become aware of them."

From: *The Candle of Vision*, by Æ
"I, with my imagination more and more drawn to adore an ideal nature, was tending to that vital contact in which what at first was apprehended in fantasy would become the most real of all things. When that certitude came, I felt as Dante might have felt after conceiving of Beatrice close at his side and in the Happy World, if, after believing it a dream, half hoping that it might hereafter be a reality, that beloved face before his imagination grew suddenly intense, vivid and splendidly shining, and he knew beyond all doubt that her spirit was truly in that form, and had descended to dwell in it, and would be with him for evermore."

"By imagination what exists in latency or essence is out-realized and is given a form in thought, and we can contemplate with full consciousness that which hitherto had been unrevealed, or only intuitionally surmised. In imagination there is a revelation of the self to the self, and a definite change in being, as there is in a vapor when a spark ignites it and it becomes an inflammation in the air. Here images appear in consciousness which we may refer definitely to an internal creator, with power to use or remold pre-existing forms, and endow them with life, motion and voice."

"The immortal in us has memory of all its wisdom. There is an ancestral wisdom in man, and we can if we wish drink that old wine of heaven. This memory of the spirit is the real basis of imagination, and when it speaks to us, we feel truly inspired and a mightier creature than ourselves speaks through us. To find sentences which seemed noble and full of melody sounding in my brain as if another and greater than I had spoken them."

"I am convinced that all poetry is, as Emerson said, first written in the heavens, that is, it is conceived by a self deeper than appears in normal life, and when it speaks to us or tells us its ancient story we taste of eternity and drink the Soma juice, the elixir of immortality."

Novalis (Friedrich von Hardenberg)

Novalis was a great inspiration for Rudolf Steiner throughout his life and during the creation of Anthroposophy. Truly, Novalis' writings carry the soul of the reader into mystical lands that seemed more real than the weight of the world and provide accurate knowledge of higher worlds. Though he died young, Novalis inspired the Romantic Movement and built a new bridge to the spirit through his crystal-clear descriptions of the sources of life, freedom, and love. Many of his works are still open secrets revealing mysteries that are ancient and futuristic all at once. There is hardly a realm of thought or experience that Novalis did not shed light upon through his inspiration and insight.

Novalis was the most significant representative of German Romanticism at the end of the eighteenth century. He was a poet, a writer, a scientist, a geologist, and a philosopher who was profoundly influenced by Fichte and Kant. The full revelation of Novalis' genius only came when his beloved Sophie von Kuhn died at age fifteen.

All of Novalis' creative works were written within the short period of three years; each of these years focused on a different area of study. The first year we see the philosopher and natural scientist at work; in the second, the writer of beautiful fairy tales and magical stories; and finally, the mystic poet of Christianity. Novalis died before he reached the age of twenty-nine.

From: *Pollen and Fragments,* by Novalis
"It is strange how our sacred history resembles a fairy tale. It commences with an evil spell, which is overcome by a marvelous expiation, and the spell is broken. I think I am best able to express my state of soul in fairy tales."

"In time, history must become a fairy tale—it shall be once again, as it was in the beginning."

"A true fairy tale must be at once a prophetic representation—an ideal representation—and an absolutely necessary representation. The true poet of the fairy tale is a seer of the future."

"The fairy tale is the canon of poesy as it were—everything poetic must be like a fairy tale. The poet worships chance."

"All novels where germinal love is presented are fairy tales—magical events. In fairy tales is my heartfelt spiritual vision best expressed."

"The fairy tale is, as it were, the canon of poetry—everything poetic must be fairylike. A fairy tale is actually like a dream-image—without coherence—an assemblage of miraculous things and events—for instance a musical fantasy—the harmonious sequences of an aeolian harp—nature herself."

"It is only because of the weakness of our organs and of our contact with ourselves that we do not discover ourselves to be in a fairy world. All fairy tales are only dreams of that familiar world of home which is everywhere and nowhere. The higher powers in us, which one day will carry out our will like genies, are now muses that refresh us with sweet memories along this arduous path."

From: *Hymns to the Night,* by Novalis
"Now I wend down to holy, ineffable, mysterious night. To us more heavenly than those radiant stars are the endless eyes that night has opened in us. But the domain of night is beyond time or space. Night has become the mighty womb of revelation."

"That will be a Golden Age, when all words become—figurative words—myths—and all figures become—linguistic figures—hieroglyphs; when we learn to speak and write figures and learn to perfectly sculpt and make music with words. Both arts belong together, are indivisibly connected and will become simultaneously perfected."

"It seems to me that a grammatical mysticism lies at the basis of everything—which could quite easily call forth the first sense of wonder with regard to language and writing. The propensity for the miraculous and mysterious is nothing more than a striving—toward nonphysical—spiritual stimuli. Mysteries are a means of nourishment—inciting potencies. Explanations are digested mysteries."

From: *The Novices of Sais,* by Novalis
"Various are the roads of man. He who follows and compares them will see strange figures emerge, figures which seem to belong to that great cipher which we discern written everywhere, in wings, eggshells, clouds and snow, in crystals

and in stone formations, on ice-covered waters, on the inside and outside of mountains, of plants, beasts and men, in the lights of heaven, on scored disks of pitch or glass or in iron filings round a magnet, and in strange conjunctures of chance. In them we suspect a key to magic writing, even grammar, but our surmise takes on no definite forms and seems unwilling to become a higher key. It is as though an alkahest had been poured over the senses of man. Only at moments do their desires and thoughts seem to solidify. Thus, arise their presentiment, but after a short time everything swims again before their eyes."

"I heard a voice say from afar that the incomprehensible is solely the result of incomprehension, which seeks what it has and therefore can never make further discoveries. We do not understand speech, because speech does not understand itself, nor wish to; the true Sanskrit would speak in order to speak, because speech is its delight and essence."

"A little later, there was one who said; 'The holy scripture needs no explanation. He who speaks true, is full of eternal life, his written word seems wondrously akin to the mysteries, for it is a chord taken from the symphony of the universe.'"

"Surely the voice was speaking of our teacher, for he knows how to gather together the traits that are scattered everywhere. A unique light is kindled in his eyes when he lays down the sacred rune before us and peers into our eyes to see whether in us the light is risen that makes the figure visible and intelligible."

The Tale of Eros and Fable from *Heinrich von Ofterdingen*, by Novalis

The Tale of Eros and Fable (Klingsor's Fairy Tale) is Novalis's answer to Goethe's fairy tale, *The Green Snake and the Beautiful Lily*. Both

Goethe and Novalis believed that fairy tales contained the most succinct wisdom found in literature. These fairy tales are created for the instruction of the aesthetic education of humanity. They are parables for the future, the currency of wisdom enchanted into images that never fade, hopeful gifts for the future of humanity.

In *The Tale of Eros and Fable*, Novalis has revisited *The Myth of Cupid and Psyche* that is embedded in *The Golden Ass*, by Apuleius, one of the most ubiquitous fairy tales. This tale is the heroine's journey of faithful love; the same theme that Novalis has reworked and raised to a new level. C. S. Lewis wrote his own version of 'Cupid and Psyche' in the book, *Until We Have Faces*. The theme of this ageless tale is truly a basis for a psychological study of love and relationships. It stands more in the German Romantic Movement as a fairy tale (marchen) than a Greek myth about Olympian destinies.

Fairy tales defy definition or literary critique and speak from an ever-present place of timelessness. Out of the night, ancient mankind found moral instruction in their commonly shared dreams. These dreams became tradition, and their meanings have almost been totally lost. Novalis reawakens in us the ability to interpret these dream-like images as forces of our own soul nature. Each character is a part of us that needs to be rediscovered. The plot is nothing less than the redemption of mankind by its own catharsis and effort. The hero/heroine is our higher self who comes to birth through understanding and transforming our lower, 'dark self.' These are 'unearthly' events that are at home in our inner life of living images, the moral imaginal realm.

As Novalis wrote about his fairy tale:–

> "The antipathy of light and shadow, the yearning for the clear, hot, penetrating ether, the unknown sanctity, the Vesta in Sophia, the mixture of the romantic elements of all ages, petrifying and petrified intellect, Arcturus. . . the spirit of life, single features as mere arabesques—it is in this light that my tale should be seen."

More than just a political allegory, *Klingsor's Fairy Tale* is a philosophical allegory of universal renewal whose encyclopedic scope of allusions bear upon the entire 'mental system of the world.'

The Tale of Eros and Fable (Klingsor's Fairy Tale)

Sophia, doomed to separation from her divine spouse, seeks ultimately to be reunited with Arcturus forever. To bring about the return of the Golden Age, Eros must be redeemed from the Realm of the Moon to awaken Freya, daughter of the gods; Fable must vanquish the Scribe, the Underworld, and the Spiders, before she can sing her song of praise to heavenly Sophia. Fable's Mother must die, and her ashes mixed with the sacred water from the altar vessel to make a healing potion for all to drink. Thus, the tale tells how Eros became the power of pure love and Fable develops the force of divine poetry, in order that Sophia, reunited with Arcturus, may become the everlasting priestess of the heart.

To 'journey to King Arcturus' Fable and Sophia simply 'climb a ladder' rapidly and go through a trapdoor in the dome of heaven to reach the chambers of King Arcturus in the starry realms. Novalis uses the simplest of space/time travel conveyances to span cosmic distances. The 'ladder' was always there, unnoticed in the corner, but awaiting the development of the traveler to be ripe enough to use it properly. Novalis shows us, many years before David Lindsay, how to travel to Arcturus in a simple fashion through Sophia's soul preparedness (catharsis and redemption) plus a humble 'ladder' to the starry heavens—Arcturus—to unite the soul (Sophia) to the higher self (the King) in a cosmic wedding beyond space and time—'and if things have not changed, they are still there today…'

Novalis is master of transcending space and time through brilliant, luminous thoughts that break the bonds of heaven and hell and bridge the chasm between the physical and spiritual (faerie) worlds. He has accomplished with his writings exactly what he has said should become of fairy tales and novels in the future—tools of personal transformation and spiritual biography. His words alone are all that is needed to travel to faerie land; they are the literary device the Inklings were looking for, the map of the 'Lost Road to the Blessed Realms.'

Through the transformation and initiation of the soul and spirit, Novalis in *The Tale of Eros and Fable*, depicts the path of spiritual development from Moral Imagination (imaginal realm) to higher realms where Moral Inspiration, as celestial music, adds to the images of the fairy tale. Once inspiration can build upon morally wise imaginations that teach lessons humanity needs to learn through spiritual development, it then becomes possible to align with the will of the divine and embody moral intuitions of love that perceive the sacred 'Lost Word' of the creator gods.

Moral Imagination, Inspiration, and Intuition (the uncontrollable desire to do the will of the good) is found throughout Novalis' inspiring work. Everywhere, the divine iridescence of the Land of Faerie lifts the reader into worlds that are spiritually alive; where many beings commune in the heavenly light, bathe in the cosmic music, and dance the cosmic will of the divine macrocosm. One can learn to live in these realms where soul renewal is found as an ever-blossoming Tree of Life and the human spirit may drink from the fountain of the eternal.

Let's listen to the way Novalis ties all suffering and redemption into a perfect resolve with some of the last lines of *The Tale of Eros and Fable*:–

> "She [Sophia] pretended to open the gate but, instead, slammed it shut noisily and slipped to the back of the cavern where a ladder hung down. She climbed it rapidly and soon reached a trapdoor which opened on the chamber of Arcturus. The King sat surrounded by his counselors when Fable appeared. The Northern Crown graced his head. In his left hand he held the Lily, in his right hand the Scales. The Eagle and the Lion sat at his feet.

"'Monarch,' said Fable, as she bowed to him respectfully: 'Hail to your well-founded throne! Glad news for your suffering heart! A speedy return of Wisdom! An eternal awakening to peace! Rest to restless love! Transfiguration of the heart! Long life to antiquity and form to futurity!'

"The King touched her with the Lily on her guileless brow. 'Whatever you ask will be granted you…'

"…Their expectation was fulfilled and surpassed. They perceived what hitherto they had lacked, and the room became an assembly of the blessed. Sophia said: "The great mystery has been revealed to all, and yet remains eternally unfathomed. The new world is born from suffering and the ashes are dissolved in tears to become the drink of eternal life. The heavenly Mother dwells in everyone, in order that each child be born eternally. Do you feel the sweet birth in the beating of your hearts?"

"The King descended from the dome, leading Sophia by the hand. The constellations and the spirits of Nature followed in glittering ranks. Inexpressibly bright daylight filled the hall, the palace, the city, and the sky. A countless throng crowded into the wide, royal hall and in silent reverence watched the lovers kneel before the King and Queen, who blessed them solemnly. The King took from his head a diadem and set it on the golden locks of Eros. The aged Hero dismantled Eros' armor, and the King wrapped his cloak around him. Then he placed the Lily in his left hand and Sophia fastened a rich bracelet over the clasped hands of the lovers. At the same time, she set her crown to Freya's brown hair.

"Finally, Sophia said: 'The Mother is among us. Her presence will gladden us forever. Follow us into our dwelling: There, in the temple, we shall dwell eternally and guard the mystery of the world. The kingdom of eternity is founded, by love and peace all strife has been impounded, the dreams of pain are gone to plague us never, Sophia is priestess of all hearts forever.'

Theosophical Thinkers with an 'Inkling' for the Spirit

In reviewing Steiner's truth aphorisms, we came across the lecture series, *The Riddles of the World and Anthroposophy* wherein he indicates that certain German thinkers have become the epitome of materialism (Kant, Haeckel, etc.), while others have unknowingly started the 'pre-school of theosophy' (Boehme, Novalis, etc.) and had already begun revealing what Steiner calls the 'cosmic wisdom of theosophy.' Many of these authors are quite familiar to us; but two held a certain special interest because of the many references to Truth discovered in their works. One author, Karl von Eckartshausen, was found to be a wealth of wisdom on all aspects of the Truth.

Even though Eckartshausen is a Christian mystic and uses many church references; his inspiration is exceptional and spurred us on to create a chapter on truth and the imaginal realms. Thus, we have accessed much truth expressed in numerous thinkers as a 'pre-school of theosophy' in that they perceived what would later become theosophy and anthroposophy.

Rudolf Steiner on Pre-Theosophical Thinkers

The selections below were taken from: *The Riddles of the World and Anthroposophy*, 22 Lectures, Berlin, October 5-May 3, 1905, GA 54, by Rudolf Steiner:–

"Of all pre-schools of theosophy or spiritual science which one can go through today the school of the German thought of the turn of the 18th to the 19th centuries is the very best for present humanity. German spiritual life of the turn from the 18th to the 19th centuries originated from the so-called Enlightenment. Great spirits developed from the Enlightenment."

"In the first half of the 19th century, even such spirits who could not go very deeply had the desire of ascending to spiritual heights, developing inner soul organs, and knew something concerning self-knowledge and self-development."

"In a theosophical way, Novalis pronounces what is a characteristic trait of that time that represented it like a theosophical spiritual motto. It is indicated in the words from Novalis' *Novices of Saïs*: "Someone succeeded; he lifted the veil of the goddess at Saïs. What did he see? He saw—miracle of miracles—himself."

"Thus, the human being comes out, after he has developed the spiritual organs in himself, and searches for himself all over the world. He does not search for himself in himself, he searches for himself in the world, and with it, he searches for God. This search of God in the world, as Novalis expresses it so nicely in the quotation above, is theosophy."

"The spiritual scientist adds, he finds the divine in his self, and this is just theosophy, divine wisdom to raise the heart, the soul to the spirit, so that one succeeds in connecting wisdom with the divine and to have not only understanding, but the general feeling of the divine world. Spiritual science is a means to give the human being food and prosperity, in the true (spiritual) sense of the word."

"Thus, it is really justified, even concerning our changed conditions, what Goethe said about the real liberation from all obstacles and misfortune of life. Goethe says in the poem *The Secrets*: "From the power that ties all beings,—that human being frees himself who overcomes himself.""

"Someone who broke with materialism definitely out of a courageous attitude was Johann Gottlieb Fichte (1762-1814). The great German thinker Fichte is to the majority a deep secret doctrine. Fichte represented the doctrine of the ego, of the human self-consciousness not speculatively, but out of the whole depth of his being."

"Fichte could speak of a special spiritual sense because he was one of those who wanted to open the eyes of human beings who are gifted with a special sense. They appear like the sighted among blind people. This sense can be evoked with every person. By the special sense, Fichte shows quite clearly that he understood theosophy. This special sense was the real definition of theosophy. Others followed from such sources, from such currents of spiritual life."

Johann Wolfgang von Goethe

Goethe produced his 'Tale of Tales' called *The Fairy Tale of the Green Snake and the Beautiful Lily* over 200 years ago and it is still as applicable today as it was then. This "extraordinary masterwork," as Friedrich Schiller called it, is unique among Goethe's works. As an initiation fairy tale of transformation, the highly symbolic story arose out of Rosicrucian-Alchemical impulses, which also play an important role in *Faust* and in Goethe's other writings. Among those influenced deeply by it was Rudolf Steiner, whose *Four Mystery Dramas* reflect some of the same themes. Both Goethe's fairy tale and Schiller's *Letters Upon the Aesthetic Education of Man* inspired Steiner to respond to these great works with his own ideas through his *Four Mystery Dramas* which he created to stage in Dornach, Switzerland, in the building he named the Goetheanum.

In June of 1786 Goethe wrote:–

> "I have read with great interest once again the old story of *The Chymical Wedding*. One day this tale will have to be told anew, but then it will have to be reborn, for it cannot be enjoyed in its old skin."

And this Goethe did when nine years later he penned the wonder fable entitled, *The Fairy Tale of the Green Snake and the Beautiful Lily*. In this work, the spiritually creative faculties of Goethe brought about an artistic metamorphosis and a profound enhancement of the Rosicrucian themes first presented in his poem *The Mysteries* (*Die Geheimnisse, The Secret Revelations*).

The artistic images comprising *The Fairy Tale of the Green Snake and the Beautiful Lily* began to appear before Goethe's creative consciousness during a journey from his home in Weimar to Karlsbad, which he made in the company of Schiller in 1795. In a letter Goethe wrote to Schiller, he said:–

> "Perhaps the idea for a fairy tale story that has come to me will develop further, but in its present form it does not entirely please me. However, if I can sail the little boat out upon the ocean of imagination, there it may yet become a fairly good composition."

In its first rendition it was called: *The Forever Glorious Fairy Tale of the Green Snake and the Beautiful Lily*. It eventually appeared in *The Hours* periodic at Michaelmas 1795 and received positive reviews that repeatedly asked Goethe to explain the meaning of *The Fairy Tale*; but alas, Goethe declined to interpret the symbols and the meaning of the characters.

Famous Quotations of Goethe

"A man sees in the world what he carries in his heart."

"All theory, dear friend, is gray, but the golden tree of life springs ever green."

"Life is the childhood of our immortality."

"Beauty is everywhere a welcome guest."

"The soul that sees beauty may sometimes walk alone."

"Few people have the imagination for reality."

"The mediator of the inexpressible is the work of art."

"There are only two lasting bequests we can hope to give our children. One of these is roots, the other, wings."

Friedrich von Schiller

Johann Christoph Friedrich von Schiller (1759–1805) was a German playwright, poet, philosopher and historian. Schiller is considered by most Germans to be Germany's most important classical playwright. During the last seventeen years of his life (1788–1805), Schiller developed a productive, if complicated, friendship with the already famous and influential Johann Wolfgang von Goethe. They frequently discussed issues concerning aesthetics, and Schiller encouraged Goethe to finish works that he had left as sketches. This relationship and these discussions led to a period now referred to as Weimar Classicism. Goethe convinced Schiller to return to playwriting. He and Goethe founded the Weimar Theater, which became the leading theater in Germany. Their collaboration helped lead to a renaissance of drama in Germany.

A pivotal work by Schiller was *On the Aesthetic Education of Man in a Series of Letters*, first published 1794, which was inspired by the great disenchantment Schiller felt about the French Revolution, its degeneration into violence and the failure of successive governments to put its ideals into practice. Schiller wrote that "a great moment has found a little people"; thus, he wrote the Letters as a philosophical inquiry into what had gone wrong, and how to prevent such tragedies in the future. In the Letters he asserts that it is possible to elevate the moral character of a people, by first touching their souls with beauty, an idea that is also found in his poem *The Artists*:–

"Only through Beauty's morning-gate, dost thou penetrate the land of knowledge."

Schiller refers in his ballad *The Veiled Image at Saïs*, to the motif of the veiled Isis, a very popular theme in artistic as well as intellectual circles at that time. It is a philosophical work theorizing the sublime and was inspired by Immanuel Kant, who used the veiled Isis of Saïs as a prime example for the sublime. Schiller's ballad is based on Plutarch's written record about a statue of Isis in the Egyptian city of Saïs, in which Plutarch states the statue bore an inscription saying:–

"I am all that has been and is and shall be; and no mortal has ever lifted my veil."

Lifting the veil of Isis is tantamount to entering the Land of Fairie where Truth, Beauty, and Goodness reside. Schiller was a true Christian theosophist whose influence on later writers cannot be over emphasized. Truly Schiller lifted the veil and beheld the beauty of Isis in nature and the human soul and spirit. We offer this poem as another example of communications with the Imaginal World from an inspired author who had an 'inkling' about a higher world filled with imaginal wisdom.

The Veiled Image at Saïs, by Friedrich von Schiller
Translated by David B. Gosselin

Struck by a burning thirst for knowledge, a youth
Travelled through ancient Egyptian lands
—to Saïs—to breach the secrets of its priests;
He eagerly made all the needed grades,
But still relentlessly kept climbing higher—
The hierophant could barely tame the boy.
"What good is one small part without the whole?"
Exclaimed the eager youth, without a pause.
"For, can the Truth be really more or less?
The way you speak of Truth is as if it
Were nothing more than a mere earthly sum,
As if a question of just more or less.
Surely, it's something whole and without parts;
The Truth is pure and indivisible!
Remove one note and harmony dissolves,
Remove one color and the rainbow fades,
And nothing will be known, so long as that
One color, or one note, remains absent.

While the priest and the eager youth conversed,
They stood amid the precincts of a temple
Where a strange statue stood silent and veiled.
It captured the excited boy's attention,
And so, he turned towards the wise old priest

And asked, "What lies hidden beneath the veil?"
"Truth," answered the old priest. "What!" said the boy,
"The Truth alone is all I care about,
And you would think of hiding it from me?"

"Only the Godhead can answer to that,"
Said the Egyptian priest. "And let no man
Reach for that veil," he said, "Until I do;
For, he who with an impure hand removes
That mystic veil and sacred covering,
'He' said the Godhead, will behold the Truth."
"How strange! And have you never tried to lift
The veil yourself, you who worship the Truth?"
"I never have, I never felt the need."
"Could it be that only a thin veil stands
Between me and the Truth of things?" he asked.
"And a divine decree," rejoined the old priest,
"The weight is heavier than you might think;
Though it may seem light to the hand—heavy—
So heavy can it weigh upon the mind."

Lost in his thoughts, the youth made his way home,
But he now burned with a desire to know.
Restless, sleepless, tossing around in bed,
He rolled for hours, until at last the clock
Struck midnight and he rose, and quietly
Found himself drawn by a powerful force.

He climbed the walls, then after one more spring,
He found himself beneath the sacred dome.

Behold! The child in utter solitude,
Stood amid nothing but the deathly silence,
A silence broken only by the echo
Of every step he took across the vault.
And through the aperture of the high dome,
The quiet moon rained down her pallid beams
Just on the place where shining in the light,
The statue stood, concealed by its long veil.

The boy began to walk towards the form:
Hesitant, he moved his impious hand
Towards the statue, and then suddenly,
A chill ran down his spine; an unseen hand
Repulsed the boy, "What do you want," echoed
A tortured voice within his shaken breast.
"Would you dare profane the Holiest One?"
"It's true, declared the oracle, 'Let none
Venture to raise the veil until I do.'
But did he not say Truth as well would rise?
Whatever it may be, I'll raise the veil."
And then he said, "I will behold the Truth!"
"Behold!"
His own words echoed back in mocking tone.

And with that word he cast the veil away.

What form his harrowed eyes met I don't know,

But when the warm, fresh morning's breeze returned,

The priests found a pale and unconscious boy

Lying before the pedestal of Isis.

He never shared what he had seen that night,

From that day on his happiness had fled;

Deep sorrow brought him to an early grave.

When pressed by questioners, he only said,

"Woe unto him, who comes to Truth through guilt:

Delight will forever be lost to him."

Friedrich von Hardenberg (Novalis)

One of those who sat at Fichte's feet and looked reverentially to him and worked out his philosophical ideas, was the young short-lived German theosophist Novalis (1772-1801). Novalis, who illumined the secrets of existence with brilliant flashes of insight, revered mathematics like a religion and was one who did lift the veil of Isis and lived.

Novalis knew how to speak in miraculous tones in his *Heinrich von Ofterdingen* about theosophy. In the *Novices of Saïs*, he shows how Hyazinth gets to know the girl Rosenblüth. In this story, a wise man comes and tells fairy tales about the magic of life, about spiritual secrets. Hyazinth and Rosenblüth become inspired by the story and decide to walk to the initiation temple of Isis. However, nobody can give them directions to the temple, and they become separated. Hyazinth walks and walks. He finally sits down, tired, among blossoming flowers and beautiful Springtime. Then, Nature speaks to him. He drops off dreaming in a ghostly way and the temple of Isis is around him. The curtain is lifted from the veiled statute, and what does he see? Rosenblüth.

Novalis describes how Rosenblüth represents that feeling of unity, that uniform idea of the whole of Nature that extends over the entire world and how one looks for the hidden secrets that life often shows to us to deepen our understanding. This is wonderfully indicated in lovely descriptions that are truly theosophic in this seemingly simple fairy tale.

Rudolf Steiner's Remarks Concerning Novalis

"And so, we see that in Novalis there lives, in a distinctively individual form, everything which has now been given through spiritual science." GA 126, *Occult History*

"Anyone who reads Novalis will feel something of the breath which leads one into this higher world. It is not expressed in the usual way, but there is something in him that charms or spells also have. They have significance as much for ordinary, undeveloped people as they have for initiates." GA 53, *The Inner Development of Man*

"Let your endeavors here be permeated as much by the spirit of Novalis as by the spirit of spiritual science itself. May such a spirit unite you, that spirit who is, at the same time, the spirit of the Masters of Wisdom." GA 272, *Goethe's Faust*

"The creative work of Novalis makes so deep an impression because whatever we have before us in immediate sense-perceptible reality, whatever the eye can see and recognize as beautiful, appears with a well-nigh heavenly splendor in the poetry of Novalis through the magical idealism that lives in his soul. Through the magical idealism of his poetry, he can make the most insignificant material thing live again in all its spiritual light and glory." GA 168, *On the Connection of the living and the Dead*

Quotations from Novalis Concerning Imagination

"The greatest good endures in the imagination."

"Reason with imagination is religion; reason with understanding is science."

"Therefore imagination, which fashions figurative words, especially deserves the predicate genius."

"The imagination places the world of the future either far above us, or far below, or in a relation of metempsychosis to ourselves. We dream of traveling through the universe—but is not the universe within ourselves? The depths of our spirit are unknown to us—the mysterious way leads inwards. Eternity with its worlds—the past and future—is in ourselves or nowhere."

"Oh! If the oracles are still at hand, then they speak from the Tree of Knowledge; thus, they sound in us; thus, we read them in the Sibylline book of nature. My fantasy rises as my hope is completely sunken and nothing remains but a marker that shows its absence, then my imagination will rise high enough to elevate me to a place where I can find what is lost down here."

"With the final stroke, the master sees his ostensible creation separated from himself by a chasm of thought, the span of which he himself scarcely comprehends, and across which only imagination, like the shadow of the giant named intelligence, can leap. At the very moment when it is to enter into full being, it becomes more than he, its creator, while he in turn becomes the organ and chattel of a higher power. The artist belongs to the work and not the work to the artist."

"The productive imagination is the beginning of a true permeation of the self by the spirit, which never ends. Without inspiration, there is no spirit-manifestation. Inspiration is manifestation and counter-manifestation, appropriation and communication all at the same time."

Ludwig Tieck

The Jena Romantics were a group of German writers, philosophers, and critics who were central to the Romantic movement and were generally all students of Johann Gottlieb Fichte, the founding figure of German Idealism. The group was active from around 1798 to 1804 and was centered in Jena, Germany. Some of the key figures in the Jena Romantic movement include:

Ludwig Tieck, August Wilhelm Schlegel, Friedrich Schlegel, Dorothea Schlegel (Friedrich's partner), Caroline Schlegel, Novalis (Friedrich von Hardenberg), Wilhelm Heinrich Wackenroder, Friedrich Schelling, and Friedrich Schleiermacher. The Jena Romantics were influenced by the older generation of writers and philosophers, including Goethe, Schiller, and Fichte. The group's periodical was entitled Athenaeum, which became the major periodical for the Jena Romantics.

Jena Romanticism, a first phase of Romanticism in German literature was centered in Jena where the group was led by the versatile writer Ludwig Tieck. Two members of the group, the brothers August Wilhelm and Friedrich von Schlegel, laid down the theoretical basis for Romanticism in the circle's periodic, the Athenaeum, maintained that the first duty of criticism was to understand and appreciate the right of genius to follow its natural bent.

The greatest imaginative achievement of this circle is to be found in the lyrics and fragmentary novels of Friedrich Leopold von Hardenberg (Novalis). The works of Johann Gottlieb Fichte and Friedrich von Schelling expounded the Romantic doctrine in philosophy, whereas the theologian Friedrich Schleiermacher demonstrated the necessity of individualism in religious thought. By 1804 the circle at Jena had dispersed. A second phase of Romanticism was initiated two years later in Heidelberg.

Ludwig Tieck (born May 31, 1773, in Berlin, Prussia [Germany]—died April 28, 1853, in Berlin) was a versatile and prolific writer and critic of the early Romantic movement in Germany. Later he became a leader of the movement and demonstrated in his writings that he was a born storyteller, and his best work has the quality of a Marchen (fairy tale) that appeals to the emotions rather than the intellect.

Tales from the Phantasus of Ludwig Tieck, is a fabulous collection of supernatural tales by Tieck. Indeed, in his prologue Tieck makes it quite clear that he is attempting to portray nature in the same extraordinary manner as Friedrich Schlegel:–

> "One does not need to go the crest of St. Gotthard to experience the sublime. These wild poems and stories will show us the awe and wonder of nature. In these kinds of stories, the beautiful mingles itself with the terrible, the sublime with the childish, goading our fancy into a kind of poetic madness, and then turning it to roam at will through the entire fabric of our souls."

Tieck's stories are wonderful and terrible all in one. When he is at his best he is on a par with the famous writers of German fantastic tales. To give a sample of Tieck's imaginal stories we share a selection from the introduction to the book, *Tales from The Phantasus of Ludwig Tieck*:–

> "'It is not at every moment, nor every time we choose to turn to her,' said Antony, 'that Nature will unfold her secrets to us; or rather, it is not always that we are in the mood to feel her sacredness. There must first be a harmony in ourselves, if we are to find what surrounds us harmonious; otherwise, we do cheat ourselves with empty phrases, without ever rising to a true enjoyment of beauty. It may be, perhaps, that there are

times when unexpectedly some blessed influence descends out of Heaven upon our hearts and unlocks the door of inspiration; but towards this we can add nothing. We have no right, no means of looking for it; it is a revelation within us we know not how. So much is certain that it is not above twice, or at most three times, in a man's life that he has the fortune, in any true sense, to see a sunrise. When we do see it, it does not pass away like a summer cloud before our minds; rather it forms one of the great epochs in our lives. From such ecstatic feelings as we receive then it is long and long ere we recover; by the side of these exalted moments years dwindle into nothingness. But it is only in the calmness of solitude that these high gifts can descend upon us. A party collecting itself to see it as a sight on the top of a mountain, is only standing as it were before an exhibition at a theatre and can bring from it nothing but the same kind of empty pleasure and foolish criticisms.'"

"'Still stranger is it,' said Ernest, 'that the great majority of men are so dead to that awe and wonder, that fearful amazement with which Nature often fills some minds. If they can feel it, it is only as an obscure bewildered sensation of they know not what.'

"'It is not only on the dreary peaks of the St. Gothard that we can feel the tembleness of Nature. There are times when the most beautiful scene is full of specters that fly shrieking and screaming across our hearts. Such strange shadowy forms, such wild forebodings, go often hunting up and down our fancy, that we are fain to fly from them in terror, and rid ourselves of our phantom rider, by plunging into the dissipations of the world. While under such influences wild poems and stories often rise up in us to people the dreary chaos of desolation and adorn it with creations of art; and these forms and figures will be unconscious betrayers of the tone and temper of the mind in which they spring. In these kinds of stories, the beautiful mingles itself with the terrible, the sublime with the childish, goading our fancy into a kind of poetic madness, and then turning it to roam at will through the entire fabric of our souls.'

"'Are the stories you are going to read to us of this kind?' asked Clara.

"'Perhaps,' replied Ernest.

"'And not allegorical?'

"'As you please to call them. There is not, and there cannot be any creation of art which has not some kind of allegory at the bottom of it, however little it may let itself be seen. The two forms of good and evil appear in every poem; they meet us at every turn, in everything man produces, as the one eternal riddle in an endless multiplicity of forms, which he is forever struggling to resolve. As there are particular aspects in which the most everyday life appears like a myth, so it is possible to feel oneself in as close connection with, as much at home in the middle of the wildest wonders as the ordinary incidents of life. One may go so far as to say, that the commonest, simplest, pleasantest things, as well as the most marvelous, can only be said to be true, can only exert an influence on our minds, in so far as they contain some allegory as their groundwork, as the link which connects them with the system of the universe. This is why Dante's allegories come so home to us, because they pierce through and through to the very heart and center of reality. Novalis says, there is no real history, except what might be fable. Of course, there are many weak and sickly poems of this kind, which merely drag wearily on to the moral, without taking the imagination along with them; and these of all the different sorts of instruction or entertainment are the most tiresome. But it is time to proceed to our tales."

Karl Wilhelm Friedrich Schlegel

Karl Wilhelm Friedrich von Schlegel (1772–1829) was a German poet, literary critic, philosopher, philologist, and Indologist. With his older brother, August Wilhelm Schlegel, he was one of the main figures of Jena Romanticism. He entered university to study law but instead focused on classical literature. He began a career as a writer and lecturer and founded journals such as *Athenaeum*. He was a promoter of the Romantic movement. Some of his works were set to music by Schubert, Mendelssohn, and Schumann.

In 1793, Schlegel devoted himself entirely to literary work. In 1796 he moved to Jena, where his brother August Wilhelm lived, and collaborated with Novalis, Ludwig Tieck, Fichte, and Caroline Schelling, who married August Wilhelm. In Jena he and his brother founded the journal *Athenaeum*, contributing fragments, aphorisms, and essays in which the principles of the Romantic school are most definitely stated. They are now generally recognized as the deepest and most significant expressions of the subjective idealism of the early Romanticists.

Famous Quotations from Friedrich Schlegel

"Wit is the appearance, the external flash of imagination. Thus its divinity, and the witty character of mysticism."

"It is peculiar to mankind to transcend mankind."

"Wit is an explosion of the compound spirit."

"Think of something finite molded into the infinite, and you think of man."

"He who does not become familiar with nature through love will never know her."

"Eternal life and the invisible world are only to be sought in God. Only within Him do all spirits dwell. He is an abyss of individuality, the only infinite plenitude."

Karl von Eckartshausen

Karl von Eckartshausen (1752-1803) was an 18th century German mystic who wrote extensively on esoteric topics. His work, *The Cloud Upon the Sanctuary*, is Christian mysticism veiled in hermetic code, Kabbalist mysteries, and ancient ideas of magic. One of his last books, *Magic—The Principles of Higher Knowledge* was one of the first books to address theosophy and anthroposophy as paths to truth. His novels, *Kosti's Journey* and also *The Hieroglyphics of the Human Heart,* are writings that are adapted to open the human soul to a higher vision of the imaginal worlds—realms filled with higher consciousness and spiritual beings.

A. E. Waite tells us about Eckartshausen in the introduction to *The Cloud upon the Sanctuary*:–

> "Apart from *The Cloud upon the Sanctuary*, Eckartshausen is a name known only to the Christian Transcendentalists of England. *The Cloud upon the Sanctuary* has, I believe, always remained in the memory of a few, and is destined still to survive, for it carries with it a message of very deep significance to all those who look beneath the body of religious doctrine for the one principle of life which energizes the whole organism. The truth of this experience being the awakening within us of a spiritual faculty cognizing spiritual objects as objectively and naturally as the outward senses perceive natural phenomenon. This organ is the intuitive sense of the transcendental world, and its awakening, which is the highest object of religion takes place in three stages: (a) morally, by the way of inspiration; (b) intellectually, by the way of illumination; (c) spiritually, by the way of revelation. The

awakening of this organ is the lifting of the 'cloud from the sanctuary,' enabling our hearts to become receptive to God, even in this world.

"We must take the key which Eckartshausen himself offers, namely, that there is within all of us a dormant faculty, the awakening of which gives entrance, as it develops, into a new world of consciousness, which is one of the initial stages of that state which he, in common with all other mystics, terms 'union with the Divine.' In that union, outside all formal sects, all orthodox bonds of fellowship, and veils and webs of symbolism, we form a great congregation, the first fruits of immortality, and in virtue of the solidarity of humanity, and in virtue of the great doctrine of the communication of all things holy with all that seeks for holiness, the 'above and the below.'"

From: *The Cloud Upon the Sanctuary,* by Karl von Eckartshausen

"Pride is the greatest atrocity in the eyes of Wisdom. It was Pride which removed mankind from the Path to the Truth, thereby obstructing access to the Temple of Nature. Truth is not for owners of Pride, but for those who seek knowledge with a sincere heart, to unselfishly help mankind."

"When all of mankind is capable of thinking in pictures or in objects, and not in symbols or signs, and we can speak in the nature of the thing and not in arbitrary signs, then we have given up our erring ways and our opinions. Then, we have reached the Kingdom of Truth."

"Love, Truth, and Purity are the sounds of the World of Spirits. They reverberate on the instrument of our Soul when the strings are harmoniously tuned."

"When the Light changes over from the Intelligence into the Will, it becomes very beneficial warmth; the same as the Good, when practiced, turns into Truth, and when the Good and Truth unite, they become Wisdom and Love."

"The true and highest Magic is the Theosophist, Knowledge of God, approximation, effectiveness through God. The second classification is the Anthroposophia, the Science of Natural Things, the Science of Human Intelligence. Let us examine the secrets of Anthroposophy, and out of the miraculousness of Nature, let us study the highest Wisdom of the Theosophist."

"Is it not true that all which we call reality is but relative, for absolute truth is not to be found in the phenomenal world."

"Love and Wisdom beget the Spirit of Truth, interior light; this light illuminates us and makes supernatural things objective to us."

"This real knowledge is actual faith, in which everything takes place in spirit and in truth. Thus, one ought to have a sensorium fitted for this communication, an organized spiritual sensorium, a spiritual and interior faculty able to receive this light; but it is closed to most men by their senses."

"With, however, the development of a new organ we have a new perception, a sense of new reality. Without it, the spiritual world cannot exist for us because the organ rendering it objective to us is not developed."

"The curtain is all at once raised, the impenetrable veil is torn away, the Cloud before the Sanctuary lifts, a new world suddenly exists for us, scales fall from the eyes, and we are at once transported from the phenomenal world to the regions of truth."

"This community possesses a School, in which all who thirst for knowledge are instructed by the Spirit of Wisdom itself;

and all the mysteries of God and of nature are preserved in this School for the children of light. Perfect knowledge of God, of nature, and of humanity are the objects of instruction in this school."

"Interior truth passed into the external wrapped in symbol and ceremony, so that sensuous man could observe, and be gradually thereby led to interior truth."

"Through these divine instruments, the interior truths of the Sanctuary were taken into every nation, and modified symbolically according to their customs, capacity for instruction, climate, and receptiveness."

"In the midst of all this, truth reposes inviolable in the inner Sanctuary."

"The society of sages communicated, according to time and circumstances, unto the exterior societies their symbolic hieroglyphs, in order to attract man to the great truths of their interior."

"The absolute truth lying in the center of Mystery is like the Sun, it blinds ordinary sight and man sees only the shadow."

"Mystic hieroglyphs are these letters also; they are sketches and designs holding interior and holy truth."

"It is to you who labor to reach truth, you who have so faithfully preserved the glyph of the holy mysteries in your temple, it is to you that the first ray of truth will be directed; this ray will pierce through the cloud of mystery and will announce the full day and the treasure which it brings."

"It is likewise with the Mysteries; their hieroglyphics and infinite number of emblems have the object of exemplifying but one single truth. He who knows this has found the key to understand everything all at once."

"The inner sensorium opens and links us onto the spiritual world. We are enlightened by wisdom, led by truth, and nourished with the torch of love."

"Before the Fall man was wise, he was united to Wisdom; after the Fall he was no longer one with Her, hence a true science through express Revelation became absolutely necessary."

We can learn from *The Cloud Upon the Sanctuary,* by Karl von Eckartshausen, that the Land of Fairie is a temple or sanctuary within ourselves that was once united with the magic world of enchantment and truth but is now lost in the illusion of the material world. The delusions caused by the sense world are what he calls 'the cloud' that covers the sanctuary, the Temple of the Divine within us that is the 'image and likeness of God.' Uncovering this pathway back to the Moral realms of the Divine is usually seen as a religious practice; but is, in fact, the road to Spirit Land, the Land of Faerie, the realms of Moral Imagination, Inspiration, and Intuition. The cloud of untruthfulness must be lifted to witness within our own hearts that paradise is regained, and that New Jerusalem is descending from the heights into the souls of humankind. This quest for the sacred sanctuary may take us along many paths and difficult journeys—*but eventually leads us back to the human heart.*

Karl von Eckartshausen is a perfect example of theosophy—the wisdom of God—transforming into anthroposophy—the wisdom of humanity. His stories of catharsis and redemption utilize religious terms to describe what Novalis, Æ, Tolkien, and Lewis describe as conquering space and time to travel to the higher worlds where eternal beauty, truth, and goodness live and reign—a sort of magical idealism incarnated. Eckartshausen's religious language attempts to 'relink' the human soul with its origins in the spirit. This is the same mission that the high-fantasy writers tried to accomplish through imaginal stories and fairy tales. Religion is derived from the Latin word *religare,* which means 'to tie fast' or to 'relink' with a stable source and foundation. Both religion and fairy stories reunite us with the original source of life, wisdom, and spirit, and then afterwards we become the 'prodigal child' who reunites with his family after separation, catharsis, and redemption. This is the message of the Inklings, who each had to struggle with their own beliefs that transformed from theosophy to anthroposophy; from the descent from the Land of Faerie, into the trials and challenges of the material world, ever carrying hope in their hearts of ascending back to their home in the spirit.

Ralph Waldo Emerson— America's Spiritual Scientist

Rudolf Steiner indicated that Americans could turn to the Transcendentalists, led by Ralph Waldo Emerson, to overcome the 'wooden doll' interpretation of Anthroposophy that is so prevalent in the United States. Steiner indicated that:–

> "America is to have a different form of Anthroposophy, and while it is presently woody and asleep, one should look to Emerson and his friends to understand it."

Thus, with the insight of a Transcendentalist who could transcend the magnetic hold that the earth beneath America has upon thinking, an American aspirant would be able to reach the higher worlds and the Land of Faerie.

American poet, essayist, and philosopher Ralph Waldo Emerson was born on May 25, 1803, in Boston, Massachusetts. After studying at Harvard and teaching for a brief time, Emerson entered the ministry. He was appointed to the Old Second Church in his native city; but soon became an unwilling preacher. Emerson was known in the local literary circle as 'The Sage of Concord.' Emerson became the chief spokesman for Transcendentalism, the American philosophic and literary movement. Centered in New England during the 19th century, Transcendentalism was a reaction against scientific rationalism. Emerson's first book, *Nature* (1836), is perhaps the best expression of his Transcendentalism, the belief that everything in our world—even a drop of dew—is a microcosm of the universe. His concept of the Over-Soul—a Supreme Mind that every man and woman share—allowed Transcendentalists to disregard external authority and to rely instead on direct experience.

Emerson's philosophy is characterized by its reliance on intuition as the only way to comprehend reality, and his concepts owe much to the works of Plotinus, Swedenborg, and Böhme. A believer in the 'divine sufficiency of the individual,' Emerson was a steady optimist. He refused to grant the existence of evil.

From: *The Natural History of the Intellect,* by Ralph Waldo Emerson

"Time was nothing; centuries and cycles were well wasted in these surveys. It seemed as if the sentences he wrote, a few sentences,—after summers of contemplation,—shone again with all the suns which had risen and set to contribute to his knowing. Few, few were the lords he could reckon, Perception, Memory, Imagination, and the sky of Reason overall. He did not know more for living long."

"For my thoughts, I seem to stand on the bank of a river and watch the endless flow of the stream floating objects of all shapes, colors and natures; nor can I much detain them as they pass, except by running beside them a little way along the bank. But whence they come or whither they go is not told me. Only I have suspicion that, as geologists say that every river makes its own valley, so does this mystic stream. It makes its valley, makes its banks, and makes, perhaps, the observer too. As soon as the intellect awakes, all things are changed; all things, the most familiar, make a musical impression."

"Perception gives pleasure; classification gives a keen pleasure. Memory does; Imagination intoxicates. See how nature has secured the communication of knowledge. And in higher activity of the mind, every new perception is attended with a thrill of pleasure, and the imparting of it to others is also attended with pleasure. Thought is the child of the Intellect, and the child is conceived with joy, and born with joy."

"Whenever the Muses sing, Pan spurts poppy juice all about, so that no one who hears them can carry any word away. So, to the Sybil's writing on leaves which the wind scatters. Alcott asked me if the thought clothes itself in words. I answer, yes, but they are instantly forgotten. The difference between man and man is that in one the memory with inconceivable swiftness flies after and recollects these leaves,—flies on wings as fast as that mysterious whirlwind, and the envious fate is baffled."

"Imagination is a spontaneous act; a perception and affirming of a real relation between a thought and some material fact. Whenever this resemblance is real, not playful, and is deep, or pointing at the causal identity, it is the act of Imagination. The very design of Imagination, this gift celestial, is to domesticate us in another nature."

"The ideal of existence is the company of a Muse who doesn't wish to wander, whose visits are in secret, who divulges things not to be made popular. Soon as the wings grow which bring the gazing eyes, even these favorites flutter too near earth. No faculty leads to the invisible world so readily as Imagination."

"Genius certifies its possession of a thought by translating it into a fact or form which perfectly represents it. Imagination transfigures, so that only the cosmical relations of the object are seen. Personal beauty, when best, has this transcendency.

Under calm and precise outline, we are surprised by the hint of the immeasurable and divine."

"Inspiration is very coy and capricious. We must lose many days to gain one, and, in order to win infallible verdicts from the inner mind, we must indulge and humor it in every way, and not too exactly harness and task it. We know vastly more than we can digest."

"Happy beyond the common lot if he learns the secret, that besides the energy of his conscious intellect, his intellect is capable of new energy by abandonment to a higher influence; or, besides his privacy of power as an individual man, there is a great Public Power on which he can draw—by only letting himself go—by a certain abandonment to it—shall I say, by unlocking at all risks his human doors, and suffering the inundation of the ethereal tides to roll and circulate through him. This ecstasy, the old philosophers called an inebriation, and said that Intellect by its relation to what is prior to Intellect is a god."

"Nothing can be done except by inspiration. The man's insight and power are local; he can see and do this, but it helps him not beyond; he is fain to make that ulterior step by mechanical means. 'Neither by sea nor by land shall thou find the way to the Hyperboreans,' said Pindar. We poorly strive by dint of time and hoarding grain on grain to substitute labor for the afflatus of Inspiration. Genius has not only thoughts, but the copula that joins them is also a thought. There's a sound healthy universe; the sky has not lost its azure because our eyes are sick."

"In domestic labor or in task work for bread, the hearing of poetry or some intellectual suggestion brings instant penitence: the thoughts revert to the Muse, and under that high invitation, we think we will throw off our chore, and attempt once more this purer, loftier service. But if we obey this suggestion, the beaming goddess presently hides her face in clouds again."

"The means of ennobling everything sensuous, and to animate also the deadest facts through uniting them to the idea, Goethe said, is the finest privilege of our super sensuous origin. Man, how much soever the earth draws him, with its thousand myriad appearances, lifts yet a searching, longing look to the heaven which vaults over him in immeasurable spaces, whilst he feels deeply in himself that he is a citizen of that spiritual kingdom, our belief in which we must not repel or surrender. In this longing lies the secret of the eternal striving after an unknown aim. It is also the lever of our searching and thinking,—soft bond between poetry and reality."

"Every man may be lifted to a platform whence he looks beyond sense perception to moral and spiritual truth;—and in that mood deals sovereignly with matter, and strings worlds like beads upon his thought. The success with which this is done can alone determine how genuine is the inspiration."

"Thought is identical with the oceanic one which flows hither and thither and sees that all are its offspring, and coins itself indifferently into house or inhabitant, into planet, man, fish, oak, or grain of sand. Nature is saturated with deity. The particle is saturated with the elixir of the universe. The thinker radiates as suns and revolves as planets."

Source of the Force—
Star Wars as Fairy Tale

I would like to share with you my personal experience of collaborating for three days in the early 70's with Marcia Lucas and a small team of anthroposophical students on the script of *Star Wars* and my discoveries about how that foundational work affected the writing, editing, and expansions of the original *Star Wars* trilogy.

First of all, it seems fitting that my first encounter with the origins of *Star Wars*—a modern fairy tale ultimately about the return to spirit—would happen at Christmas time, a season in which humanity recalls its sense of spirit and hope. It was, in a strange way, a Christmas gift of spirit wisdom that ultimately brought the light of spirit and the 'life force' into modern materialistic consciousness. Even throughout the endless battles and 'star wars' highlighted in the movies, the true, the beautiful, and the good are ultimately victorious as love eventually wins the day.

I was a student at the Waldorf Institute at the time, and I clearly remember the day that I first heard of the characters of Luke Skywalker, R2D2, C3PO, and the entire Star War's entourage. Yet, when I first encountered them, they were more like two-dimensional paper-dolls in an unfinished script before the think-tank breathed life into the plot and characters. For example, Luke Starkiller (original name) as I met him was a far cry from the Luke Skywalker he turned out to be. You may be surprised to learn that the entire story in its original form was 'seen' through the eyes of two robots and was basically flat and rather dull. The characters were not yet the familiar, crowd-pleasing heroes and heroines who would become some of the most famous and endearing characters in movie history. That is, of course, before some Waldorf teacher training students and I spent three days as part of a think-tank with George Lucas' talented wife and professional film editor, Marcia Lucas (née Marcia Griffin), to transform a silly story into a sweeping modern sci-fi, space fairy tale musical that evokes a timeless sense of heroics, redemption, and ascension.

Meeting Marcia

At that time, like the characters of the treatment, I was in development also, as are all earnest students of the spirit. In addition to being a student of Anthroposophy—a discipline of knowledge developed by Rudolf Steiner concerned with all aspects of human life, spirituality, and future evolution—I also managed the Waldorf Institute bookstore, which held a treasure trove of spiritual knowledge. That Christmas season had been busy, and I was just locking up the store and getting ready to head home when my teacher, Werner Glas, approached me.

Born in Austria, Werner was a beloved instructor at the Waldorf Institute and arguably the most prominent scholar of Anthroposophy in America. I can still say today that it was a great honor to be his student. That day, there was a glint of lighthearted cheer in his eyes. Thinking that he was simply going to wish me a Merry Christmas, I was surprised when he asked me to follow him.

"Where?" I said, blindly following him like a faithful puppy.

Without answering, he led me into one of the more spacious classrooms, where three other students were already seated around a table, talking with the Institute's co-director, Hans Gebert. A woman I did not recognize seemed to be at the center of the conversation—a pleasant looking brunette with a friendly yet sophisticated air. When everyone saw Werner in the doorway, they looked up with a sense of expectation, as most students typically did when Werner walked into a room. He was like a father to us all. He motioned me to take a seat, then sat down and began to explain the situation.

"I'm very pleased to introduce you all to Marcia Lucas," he said. "Her husband is a well-known movie director who is working on a screenplay for a science fiction film—a space opera of sorts—and they would like our Waldorf perspective. I don't know if you have heard of George Lucas?"

This was the first time I had ever heard George Lucas' name. I certainly hadn't seen his critically acclaimed and commercially successful movie *American Graffiti*. I also didn't know that his wife, Marcia, was an accomplished film editor in her own right.

Werner continued: "Well, Marcia is familiar with Anthroposophy and the work of Rudolf Steiner, and she needs our help with her husband's movie treatment to make it more Waldorf-inspired so it will have good merit as both a movie and a spiritual story."

Marcia nodded and offered more context. She said that the 'big screen' should be used to deliver important messages to audiences and tell a spiritual story, one that has a strong foundation in truth, not just another director's fantasy.

This began to inspire me because storytelling is at the center of our curriculum in Waldorf schools. Movies are mass exposure to stories. Stories, like fairy tales, help inspire the psyche of those who hear them, somewhat like collectively shared dreams. At any typical Waldorf school, teachers tell stories to the children by heart. The next day, the children retell the story from their own memory. The classroom lessons are taught like an oral tradition. Once the stories are memorized by the children, they are further elaborated on through music, dance, illustrations, paintings, or any number of other creative responses to the content of the story.

Marcia needed our input because the script was entering its third draft treatment and lacked an element of spirituality and deeper meaning and had been rejected twice by the film studio. I could see that her intent was to ask us to help her problem-solve the situation she and her husband were in. She was earnestly searching for a way to make the screenplay work because the studio had already told them they would fund two movies with them because of their success with the movie *American Graffiti*. The studio had already rejected the first two treatments that had been submitted. This third attempt had to be right.

"I'm sure we're up to the task," Werner said, looking at me.

For the past few minutes, I had been sitting there wondering, "Why am I here? No one told me about this meeting." Then, I looked around and realized that I was the most experienced student there. The others were too young, less studied in Anthroposophy and certainly not up to this level of work. I was immensely relieved that Werner would be there to lead us through the sessions, so I sat back and relaxed.

"The dialogue is a bit lacking," Werner said. "I told Marcia we could help with those issues as well."

With that, Werner rose from his seat and said, "Well, then. My family is waiting at home, and I must be off."

None of us could believe it. The leading Anthroposophist in America was going to leave this important project in our hands?

Werner added, "Douglas is my right-hand man. You are in good hands. I will check in on your progress as I am able throughout the next few days." He smiled that inimitable smile that was mischievous and yet 'all knowing.'

He then welcomed Marcia to the resources and hospitality of the Institute and politely left.

With Werner gone, we all looked at the Institute's co-director, the Viennese physicist Hans Gebert, to lead the session.

Hans stood up. "Well, I must admit that science and mathematics are my true specialty," Hans said, in his sprightly fashion. "So, I am afraid I will not be of much assistance to this group." He politely bid us all adieu and left.

At this point, I panicked. *My leaders had led me into the great unknown!* Marcia Lucas, who I did not know at the time was one of the greatest film editors in the world, was looking expectantly at me.

I suddenly got the feeling Werner had said something to her about me, akin to his comment about me being his 'right hand man.' I had a realization that both she and I were here solely because of Werner. Having been a brilliant actor at the London School of Theater, Werner had been the leading Anthroposophist at the North Hollywood Waldorf school who was constantly interacting with actors, directors, and producers. Marcia was here because of Werner, and I was here because he had brought a promising student to the table for this specialized project. Surely, he knew what he was doing, so I decided to trust the situation. "Well, then, let's get started," I said. "Tell us the story, Marcia."

As she spoke, I got up and went over to the classroom blackboard. Marcia had trouble articulating the story because it didn't flow easily. In colored chalk, I began to sketch out a mind-map and a storyboard of what she read to us.

"It's a story of two robots. In essence the viewer sees the entire movie through their eyes," she said. "The robots are key elements of the story. They must be kept."

I understood that the robots were non-negotiable. We must somehow work with them. "Ok," I said. "Can you please read us the starting dialogue?"

She began. It was difficult for us to listen to. As an experienced editor, Marcia knew this. The characters didn't work. They weren't alive. She sincerely wanted to rewrite her husband's movie script to its fullest potential; but at this moment, it was stilted and dry. Only later would I learn more about the context of their partnership—how George was a genius concerned with the theme of machines and technology, and Marcia was the spiritual side, focused on telling a meaningful story that would resonate with the audience. I did not know it then—*but she was here at our school trying to save the script.*

I decided to be frank with her. "First, the story is not archetypal," I said. "The author doesn't know the true nature and value of the characters he is set on 'gluing' together." Marcia began writing down notes quickly in her notebook. I continued, "The dialogue is unreal and trite. It serves only one purpose—to move to the next scene. So, I can see that the message of the story happens in the action between scenes." She nodded and kept writing notes. "There is no character development. No one will identify with these characters," I said abruptly.

Then, on a positive note: "However, your husband has tapped into the true spiritual reality of our time. His obsession to 'see' the world through the eyes of two robots is genius; but a little confusing. We can work with that."

Since everyone there, including Marcia, was a student of Anthroposophy, I began to do what Werner knew would come naturally to me as both a teacher and a student—apply the principles that I had studied to our current problem with the script.

"George has described the challenge of our times," I said, "The war with machines, symbolized in the two robot playmates of Luke Starkiller."

Now, an interesting side note about the names. Like Luke Starkiller, none of the character's names that Marcia read to us were in their final form. In fact, I later recommended that the hero, Luke Starkiller, be changed to 'Lucas Skywalker,' derived from American Indian and Tibetan traditions. Then, since Lucas is the name for 'light,' I also had the concept of a light saber, a weapon that both defends as a shield and returns attacks as a formidable and undefeatable force. In anthroposophical terms, the light saber represents the human frontal spinal column and its chakras and the gland system, especially the pineal gland. Those details would come later. But for now, we had to focus on shaping the story itself.

"I think it needs to be written like a fairy tale," I said, explaining that all fairy tales begin with a reference of the story being outside of 'time and space' in a realm of 'once upon a time in a land far, far away' and ends with some reference to their own continuance, 'and if things have not changed they are still there today.'

"I think what you may want is an adult science-fiction fairy tale opera that is spiritually accurate, yet engrossing and interesting." I offered. Marcia agreed.

With her input, we decided to begin with Luke Starkiller. We tried to describe his character development in terms of the polarity that every person has in their soul—the left and right-hand paths of evil. In the end, it is the middle path, the 'life force,' that the Jedi warrior should choose. Yet, without exploring both the left and right paths, the Jedi is weakened by not understanding his enemy.

"So, each movie goer will be faced with making the same decision, no matter what their life is like?" said one of the students.

"Yes, that's the path of most fairy tales," I said. The question is: "Which of the three paths will you choose?"

Here again, I was impressed with George Lucas' brilliance. His obsession with machines underscored the biggest challenge of our age—the right-hand path of mechanical occultism as described by Rudolf Steiner, and the left-hand path of thinking that has turned evil. Had I seen his first film, THX 1138, I would have recognized this even sooner.

"The two robots can represent thinking and willing," I proposed.

As the heroes of George's original story, both C3PO and R2D2 enable the audience to 'see through the eyes of machines.' In his relationship and interactions with the two robots, Luke uses them to enhance his thinking (C3PO) and willing (R2D2) in an age of machines; but finally finds the middle path of feeling and ultimately love.

"Let's explore the two extremes, the left-hand path of thinking and the right-hand path of willing," I said. We spent time talking it through. Both C3PO and the Evil Emperor are on the left-hand path of 'thinking' that has turned evil. For example, C3PO can think with artificial intelligence but is always afraid to act, and the Evil Emperor's well thought out plans need Darth Vader's dominate willpower to carry out. In contrast, R2D2 and Darth Vader are on the right-hand path of 'willpower.' Even though they have the capacity to will, they still need to be told what to do. They act out of duty and compulsion, not freedom.

"Darth Vader is the being we know as Ahriman," I added. "He represents the composite cleverness of all machines, incarnated into a human being. He needs to be a cyborg who is half man and half machine who is torn between the two sides of his personality."

"So, what about a middle path? Is there one?" one of the students asked.

"Excellent question," I said. "The middle path is what both the right-hand and left-hand paths miss and can't comprehend. Unable to understand the middle path, both sides seek to destroy it. The Jedi masters such as Obi-Wan Kenobi have developed themselves through the middle path, having already mastered and rejected the other two evil paths. They represent the needed balance between the two extremes."

Indeed, this dynamic of two poles of evil is the central motif of the first *Star Wars* installments.

Lord of the Machines

Once we understood the story in context of this Anthroposophical framework, the next step was to focus further on Luke's character. "I think that Luke needs to develop his character by interacting with the two robots, both the left and the right-hand paths," I said.

We then discussed each robot. As a robot on the 'thinking' side, C3PO can speak many languages and is programmed for etiquette and translating. He represents an evil that has been around as long as the many different languages in every culture since the beginning of human intellectual development and the Fall of the Tower of Babel. The confusion of languages was a trick of the being named Lucifer, who incarnated in a physical body in China in 2,000 B.C. As the 'left-hand path of evil,' Lucifer is a promethean archetype who brings fire, language, philosophy, writing and culture to humanity. Chained to a mountain, his willpower was imprisoned by the angry gods. He suffered each day as a vulture ate his liver. Eventually he was rescued by

Heracles. So, by representing Lucifer/Prometheus as the robot C3PO, this would serve as a counter-pole to the incarnation, four thousand years later around 2,000 A.D., of Ahriman, the lord of machines, otherwise known as 'Darth Vader.'

Luke, who models the original Heracles, or the hero in all of us, eventually breaks the chains to free Prometheus, the fire-bringer, who is on the left-hand path. So, too, the Evil Emperor in *Star Wars* represents the power of fire, seen as lightning shooting from his hands. He also represents Lucifer's fall from heaven since he adopted the evil wisdom of the Sith that increasingly consumes him as he misuses his powers.

"Luke is situated between the two robots, between the two paths, like his twin sister Leia. His spirituality is drawing him upward into spirit just as it does with Leia," I said.

All Jedi warriors have transformed blood, what was later called 'midi-chlorian in the blood.' As Jedis balance the forces of the left and right paths, they raise consciousness, which then increases the spiritual potential in the blood, a process that Rudolf Steiner calls the 'etherization of the blood.' As Steiner taught, spiritual people charge their blood with a consciousness that connects them to spirit (life force). However, unlike the movie, the ability to access spirit or the 'life force' isn't passed along through heredity and the blood.

After discussing all these concepts and laying the groundwork for a common understanding amongst the participants of this think-tank, here is the story of *Star Wars* that we mapped out:

Once upon a time, in a galaxy far, far away, Luke Skywalker (the archetypal human) finds his life embroiled, if not consumed, by machines. Luke is the master of those machines because he has consciousness and, therefore, is pulled by the left- and right-hand powers that machines provide. He is an orphan, as all modern souls find themselves, and knows that something great lives inside of him. He has hope in a hopeless world.

Luke's father has fallen prey to the evil right-hand path of machines that transforms him into a half-man half-machine abomination who wars against his own spirit and wishes to dominate the world, even if it means killing his son and daughter.

The left-hand path of personal black magic lives in the Evil Emperor who also wishes to kill all Jedi and, most especially, the son of Darth Vader because he knows he is a great threat to the Evil Empire.

Luke is protected by the humble Jedi, Obi-Wan Kenobi. Eventually, Obi-Wan teaches Luke the path of the 'middle way' (life force) and ultimately sacrifices himself for Luke so that he can help him from the spiritual world. The middle path is the key to developing Luke's higher self and mastering the 'life force' for the good and moral work of the Jedi.

On the path, just like Dorothy on the Yellow Brick Road, Luke gains some traveling companions. Just as the *Wizard of Oz* was a distillation of Masonic initiation rituals and meant to be an allegory on the modern banking system, *Star Wars* introduces the audience to the three parts of the soul and their inherent capacities. This is necessary to make the story more archetypal, so that the story line will always remain fresh.

For example, Obi-Wan Kenobi represents the highest of the three parts of the soul, the consciousness soul, which merges spirit with matter, just as his Jedi capacities give him the power of 'mind over matter.'

Chewbacca represents the lower soul, the sentient or astral soul that must turn the animal in us into a human being with spiritual characteristics.

Han Solo represents the intellectual soul that first begins to awaken through cleverness and then to higher thinking. Although clever, Hans lacks the ability to see the big picture like Obi-Wan Kenobi.

Between Luke's three companions, much like the Scarecrow, Tin Man, and Lion, each companion teaches a special quality to Luke along the way. Rudolf Steiner calls these soul qualities 'thinking, feeling, and willing.'

At the center of the story, Luke represents the ego, or the conscious human being who must master the three steps of the development of the soul—sentience, intelligence, and consciousness.

A Return to Spirit

Now that we had built the underlying framework, which was the most Herculean part of our task, it was clear to me that we needed to develop these characters into archetypes. Knowing now what motivated each character, we could easily hear the words that each would naturally say and even envision their realistic reactions to the unfolding plot since they were archetypes of the human soul and spirit.

In doing so, we kept in mind a fundamental truth: good and evil are choices. The Evil Emperor and Darth Vader were not born evil; they chose their own paths. Luke, the archetypal human, also must make his choices and live with the good or evil that results.

Still, after all the work we had done, one thing was missing. "We still have one problem," I reminded Marcia. "Where is Luke going in the story?" Sorely missing in the original version of the story, this issue had to be resolved so that everything else would make sense.

"Isn't Luke, essentially, the prodigal son?" I asked. Others agreed that Luke was separated from his parent's home and longing to return. This is a universal element with which every person can identify. Like Luke, each of us has our destiny. In our life, we embark on the search to find it and return to our kingdom in the spirit. We further developed Luke's direction and role in the story as follows: Luke knows he is special but doesn't know why. Throughout the story, he must evolve into his mission of facing his true identity as Darth Vader's son, accept it, and decide what to do about it.

Ultimately, Luke denies the power of the machines that try to gain control over him. Instead of the cold-hearted machine-human hybrids, Luke chooses love, freedom, and moral duty. He must come to this awakening only after receiving help from his companions. Ultimately,

Luke decides to go to the original temple of the Jedi and live under the World Tree whose leaves have the wisdom of the Cosmos inscribed upon them and are collected and placed into the sacred books the Jedi kept in the temple. From there, he turns from war and fighting to transcendence with the help and love of his sister, his friends, and his master.

Luke's sister Leia (who I suggested should be called Maya) represents his spiritual self. Although first drawn to her through physical desire, Luke transforms this attraction into spiritual love and links his destiny to hers, as the soul links to the spirit.

Leia is much surer of herself and had been treated like a princess throughout her life. Luke struggles to 'catch up' to Leia's development; but in the end, their destinies are permanently entwined, and they need each other to ascend as they both join together under the World Tree. Luke is on the spiritual path of self-development versus the physical path of earthly gratification and doesn't 'win the girl'; that part of the story is left to other characters like Han Solo and Leia who have a child who continues the Jedi tradition as an enlightened woman and a wise priestess, not a warrior.

As part of his journey, Luke uses the middle path of the 'life force' to conquer both the Evil Emperor and Darth Vader. The more the left and right-hand paths try to win Luke, the more they fall prey to the side-effects of using evil for personal gain.

As the modern human being, Luke conquers the evil machine-like foes with help from his companions and develops two powerful capacities that the machines cannot control: human freedom and love. In this way, Luke learns to 'see through the eyes of machines' and ultimately understands and conquers evil. He even sacrifices his hand to deny his father's attempt to win him over to the Dark Side of the machine world.

In the end, Luke loves his father and witnesses his death, after Vader kills the Evil Emperor. Darth Vader dies in Luke's arms and they both reconcile knowing that they still love one another. This is the same modern challenge that each of us faces: Who are your parents? Are you the same as your parents? What do you choose: the physical world of machines or the middle path of the spirit, the life force? What is your destiny?

A Beautiful Fairy Tale

Over the next two days, we built on our initial framework and polished the ideas to represent every possible perspective in our archetypal science-fiction prodigal-son fairy tale. The script was turned into a beautiful fairy tale that I was certain had merit, whether it ever made it to the big screen or not. I was very happy to work through these concepts with Marcia because I could see my own path to the spirit unfolding in the story. I assumed that Werner already understood that this would be a component of my involvement. He was always far-sighted in his understanding.

I also appreciated Marcia's priority of effective storytelling. In modern times, I have seen a decline of storytelling in our culture. This is dangerous, for as archetypal stories vanish, our imagination weakens as the source of inner nourishment and soul inspiration. Movies have taken the place of storytelling and actors have taken the place of the heroes and heroines found in all archetypal stories, whether they are derived from myth, religion, legend, fairy tale, fable, or any other transcendental source of inspiration. Yet, as we learned in developing *Star Wars*, if a story is not archetypal, it will not pass the test of time. Still very successful to this day, forty years after it was released, the archetypal story of *Star Wars* has proven the test of time as an archetypal fairy tale.

After our work was completed, I said good-bye to Marcia and wished her well with the movie. She thanked me and everyone else who had contributed their ideas to our marvelous fairy tale. I heard nothing more until 1977, when the movie was about to launch and was generating a frenzied furor of media attention.

I was working in the bookstore when Werner Glas came in to tell me the news: Marcia and George Lucas were so happy with our help that they were offering all Waldorf schools in the U.S. a chance to show an advanced screening of the movie as a local fundraiser. This was a thrilling offer, because I knew that a good deal of money could be raised. Yet, staying true to its practice of opposing TV, movies, and technology in general, the Waldorf Institute and the Waldorf school movement in America politely declined the offer, to my deep disappointment.

I finally finished watching *Star Wars*, after waiting impatiently for all nine installments, and was happy that it stayed somewhat true to the fairy tale idea we had developed in our Waldorf think-tank.

As I watched the movies, I realized that *Star Wars* had affected the paths of those of us involved in the project. Just as we had mapped out a path for Luke, we were all on a journey to our own destinies. The archetypes we built had done their work.

For example, by working through the philosophical concepts, I saw my own path to the spirit reflected in the story, as Werner knew would happen—the process had further emboldened my own understanding of anthroposophy. Also, I remembered that Werner, who was like a scholarly father, had introduced me to Marcia as his 'right hand man,' and that Luke Skywalker had sacrificed his own right hand in the battle with his father—both situations connected to the pursuit of spiritual knowledge. As a 'right hand man' for Werner in the project with Marcia, I started to grow into my leadership role as a Waldorf teacher and teacher trainer. So too, with the substitution of his right hand, Luke acquired a more masterful poise as a 'wise' Jedi warrior who had successfully denied the Dark Side and become more in touch with the 'life force.'

George Lucas himself was on the path to his genius in commercial and merchandizing success. He would later open his famous Skywalker Ranch, which I think is a much better name than 'Starkiller' Ranch, don't you?

Yet, when his own right hand, Marcia Lucas, was symbolically severed in their 1983 divorce, he lost a part of the spirituality that had been evident in the earlier movies and some say lacking in the later installments of the *Star Wars* series.

For her part, Marcia Lucas would stand on stage to be ceremoniously honored, just like the characters at the ending of *Star Wars*. Looking tasteful and quietly elegant next to a glittering presenter, Farrah Fawcett, at the 1977 Academy Awards, Marcia accepted an Oscar for best editing of a film. A humble film that started off an as unknown children's space opera ultimately became a 'household name' and the most lucrative movie endeavor of all time. At that ceremony, one of her editor colleagues would speak for her, and she would not have an opportunity to thank anyone publicly, not even her husband. Had they given her a chance at the microphone, I imagine that Marcia perhaps might have thanked the Waldorf Institute, although the process of being involved in this influential project was, for me, its own reward.

In fact, later, when working with producer Kathleen Kennedy during the creation of the Indiana Jones movies, I was quite aware of my participation in shaping small moments in these movies where true wisdom and light shine through the story. This is what I have tried to do in all of my writings; share the love for spirit that I try to live each day and to bring that spirit into the souls of everyone I have the privilege to meet or touch in some small way—even through a simple story that is the ubiquitous retelling of the original story of humanity, *the return to spirit*.

Just a few days ago, with all the resurgence of *Star Wars* memories and the recent release of the latest installment in the series, I googled Marcia Lucas' name and discovered that she and George had divorced in 1983. She had returned to using her maiden name, Marcia Griffin. When I worked with her, I had no idea that she was one of the greatest film editors in the world, her skills having been regularly in demand by the top directors, including Scorsese and Coppola. I was delighted to learn about her Academy Award and believe she is an unsung heroine in the history of *Star Wars*. After all, how often does a mortal human being create something eternal—a story that lasts forever?

Conclusion

We have been blessed to have the inspired wisdom of the Inklings that take us from the nebulous realm of theosophy (wisdom of God) to the clear thinking of anthroposophy (wisdom of humans). Whether through contrivances of space and time travel, or through the comprehensive cosmology of anthroposophy which also defies space and time, we all need to know the origin of our spirit-home and find the path back to where we can become re-united with our rightful inheritance: truth, beauty, and goodness. This path is described in timeless fairy tales, the high-fantasy of the Inklings, and the writings of the magical idealists who recount the spiritual nature of our past and point in the direction of our future development—from 'once upon a time' to 'if things have not changed, they are still there today.'

It is important to remember that the inspiration for many of the greatest stories of our time arose from the wisdom of theosophy and anthroposophy. The Inklings had an 'inkling' or 'notion' that they were more than physical, material human beings bound to the earth and that they inherently knew there are imaginal kingdoms of wonder and enchantment above the realms of this earthly world. Whether through a spaceship, a magic stone from Solomon' crown, an enchanted ladder to heaven, or the beautiful words and images of great writers, humans can and do transcend space and time with consciousness.

There is a longing for spirit that nothing but communion with the spirit can satisfy. As we read Tolkien's *Lord of the Rings* trilogy, or Lewis' Space trilogy, something is insinuated into our soul that there is 'more to life' than the drudgery and suffering we all go through—that there is an eternal spiritual realm calling our name and beckoning us forward into a brighter future. We might eventually come to understand that somewhere there is a magic star we can put on our forehead that opens supersensible organs of perception into other worlds that interpenetrate our material world. Somehow, the seeker of truth on the quest to higher knowledge can find the hidden trace back to their home in the lands beyond the earth, the ocean, the sky. It is our own refined soul and spirit qualities that know if what we 'imagine' is true or not, if those qualities are founded in moral virtues and love for humans and the divine. A simple *Grimms' Fairy Tale* may hold the secret to the Holy Grail; or perhaps, it is simply a silly children's story worth no account—the insight needed to determine the truth is up to us. If we could develop the supersensible, imaginative capacities of Novalis, Æ, or Rudolf Steiner, then every stone or leaf would display ineffable wisdom whose depth cannot be fathomed by normal sense perception or earth-bound thought. Indeed, spiritual and elemental beings permeate all of nature, but seeing them is another story that might require using some 'faerie dust' to transcend space and time.

We have attempted to demonstrate that whether some modicum of spiritual inspiration for the Inklings' stories came from Rudolf Steiner's anthroposophy, or whether the Inklings were like other great theosophers who took their ideas from myths, religions, revelations, or direct intuition, these great writers revealed universal wisdom through the enchanted beauty and moral goodness of their stories. These inspired magical idealists are the forerunners of human development who have nurtured supersensible organs of perception that were able to witness the imaginal realms from which come archetypal creative forces bringing illumination to the imagination, beauty and divinity to inspiration, and virtuous moral lessons of the spirit into human intuition. One might call these writers 'initiates of the spirit,' who guide humanity upward on the path back home to the origins of the human spirit. Each of us are on a similar sojourn and can recognize and resonate with the timeless wonder-tales of writers who have an 'inkling of the spirit.' The transcendent loving spirit in our heart recognizes the revelations of others through intuitions that nourish the soul and spirit.

Conclusion

Once we witness a description of that familiar wellspring of intuition, it is incumbent upon the questing soul to find their unique path to the summit of the spiritual mountain and to realize that their personal biographical tale of destiny can be turned into a fairy tale where they ultimately 'live happily ever after.'

BIBLIOGRAPHY

- Gabriel, Tyla. *The Gospel of Sophia: The Biographies of the Divine Feminine Trinity,* Volume Our Spirit, Northville, 2014.

- Gabriel, Tyla. *The Gospel of Sophia: A Modern Path of Initiation,* Volume 2. Our Spirit, Northville, 2015.

- Gabriel, Tyla and Douglas. *The Gospel of Sophia: Sophia Christos Initiation,* Volume 3. Our Spirit, Northville, 2016.

- Gabriel, Douglas. *The Spirit of Childhood.* Trinosophia Press, Berkley, 1993.

- Gabriel, Douglas. *Goddess Meditations.* Trinosophia Press, Berkley, 1994.

- Gabriel, Douglas. *The Eternal Curriculum for Wisdom Children: Intuitive Learning and the Etheric Body.* Our Spirit, Northville, 2017.

- Gabriel, Douglas. *The Eternal Ethers: A Theory of Everything.* Our Spirit, Northville, 2018.

- Gabriel, Douglas. *Hidden History of the Grail Queens.* Our Spirit, Northville, 2019.

- Gabriel, Douglas. *The Spirit of Childhood*: The Waldorf Curriculum. Our Spirit, Northville, 2024.

- Gabriel, Douglas. *Intuitive Learning: Activating the Well-springs of Giftedness.* Our Spirit, Northville, 2023.

The Series: *From the Works of Dr. Rudolf Steiner*

- Gabriel, Douglas. *The Incarnation of Ahriman: The Occult Annihilation of the Soul.* Our Spirit, Northville, 2023.

- Gabriel, Douglas. *How to Become An Angel: Preparing for the Future Sixth and Seventh Epochs.* Our Spirit, Northville, 2023.

- Gabriel, Douglas. *Surviving Apocalypse: Creating Your Ark.* Our Spirit, Northville, 2023.

- Gabriel, Douglas. *Life After Death: Steiner's Book of the Dead.* Our Spirit, Northville, 2023.

- Gabriel, Douglas. *The Second Coming of Christ in the Etheric Realm.* Our Spirit, Northville, 2024.

- Gabriel, Douglas. *Grappling with Evil: Conquering Fear and Anxiety.* Our Spirit, Northville, 2024.

- Gabriel, Douglas. *The Human Heart: Supersensible Organ of Perception.* Our Spirit, Northville, 2024.

- Gabriel, Douglas. *Anthroposophia: The Divine Feminine Trinity.* Our Spirit, Northville, 2024.

- Gabriel, Douglas. *Spiritual Enlightenment and Initiation.* Our Spirit, Northville, 2024.

- Gabriel, Douglas. *Cosmic Intelligence and Spiritual Hierarchies.* Our Spirit, Northville, 2024.

- Gabriel, Douglas. *Developing Christ in Our Threefold Ego.* Our Spirit, Northville, 2024.

- Gabriel, Douglas. *The Eighth Sphere: Evil and Devolution.* Our Spirit, Northville, 2024.

Recommended Reading

- A.E., (George William Russell), *The Avatars: A Futurist Fantasy*, London: Macmillan, 1933.

- Anderson, Douglas A., *Tales Before Narnia, The Roots of Modern Fantasy and Science Fiction*, Ballantine Books, 2008.

- Barfield, Owen, *Saving the Appearances*, Faber and Faber, 1965.

- Barfield, Owen, *The Rose on the Ash-Heap*, Barfield Press, UK, 2009.

- Barfield, Owen, *The Silver Trumpet*, Barfield Press, UK, 1969.

- Barnwell, John. *The Arcana of the Grail Angel: The Spiritual Science of the Holy Blood and of the Holy Grail.* Verticordia Press, Bloomfield Hills, 1999; 2nd ed. 2024.

- Barnwell, John. *The Arcana of Light on the Path: The Star Wisdom of the Tarot and Light on the Path.* Verticordia Press, Bloomfield Hills, 1999; 2nd ed. 2024.

- Goethe, Johann Wolfgang von, *Goethe: The Collected Works*, Volume 10, *Conversations of German Refugees*, Princeton Press, 1995.

- Goethe, Johann Wolfgang von, *Fairy Tale of the Green Snake and the Beautiful Lilly*, Rudolf Steiner Publications, New York, 1979.

- Harwood, A. C., *The Way of a Child*, Rudolf Steiner Press, 1969.

- Hilty, Palmer, *Henry von Ofterdingen*, by Novalis, Waveland Press, 1990.

- Lewis, C. S., *The Dark Tower and Other Stories*, HarperCollins, New York, 1977.

Bibliography

- Lewis, C. S., *The Screwtape Letters*, HaperCollins, New York, 1942.

- Lewis, C. S., *The Discarded Image*, Cambridge University Press, 1964.

- Lindsay, David, *A Voyage to Arcturus*, Allison and Busby, London, 1965.

- Llanfynydd, Carmarthen. *Klingsohr's Fairy Tale*, by Novalis, Unicorn Books, 1974.

- Manheim, Ralph, *The Novices of Sais*, by Novalis, Archipelago Books, 2005.

- Morelli, Luigi, *J.R.R. Tolkien, Owen Barfield and the Cosmic Christ*, iUniverse, 2019.

- Rosencreutz, Christian, *The Chymical Wedding of Christian Rosencreutz Anno 1459*, St. George Publications, New York, 1981.

- Tolkien, J.R.R., *Tales from the Perilous Realm*, HarperCollins, Great Britain, 1997.

- Tolkien, J.R.R., *The Lost Road and Other Writings*, Del Rey, New York, 2020.

- Williams, Charles, *The Figure of Beatrice*, Apocryphile Press, 2005.

- Williams, Charles, *Many Dimensions*, Street Write, Simplicissimus Book Farm.

ABOUT DR. RUDOLF STEINER

Rudolf Steiner was born on the 27th of February 1861 in Kraljevec in the former Kingdom of Hungary and now Croatia. He studied at the College of Technology in Vienna and obtained his doctorate at the University of Rostock with a dissertation on Theory of Knowledge which concluded with the sentence: "The most important problem of human thinking is this: to understand the human being as a free personality, whose very foundation is himself."

He exchanged views widely with the personalities involved in cultural life and arts of his time. However, unlike them, he experienced the spiritual realm as the other side of reality. He gained access through exploration of consciousness using the same method as the natural scientist uses for the visible world in his external research. This widened perspective enabled him to give significant impulses in many areas such as art, pedagogy, curative education, medicine, agriculture, architecture, economics, and social sciences, aiming towards the spiritual renewal of civilization.

He gave his movement the name of "Anthroposophy" (the wisdom of humanity) after separating from the German section of the Theosophical Society, where he had acted as a general secretary. He then founded the Anthroposophical Society in 1913 which formed its center with the construction of the First Goetheanum in Dornach, Switzerland. Rudolf Steiner died on 30th March 1925 in Dornach. His literary work is made up of numerous books, transcripts and approximately 6000 lectures which have for the most part been edited and published in the Complete Works Edition.

Steiner's basic books, which were previously a prerequisite to gaining access to his lectures, are: *Theosophy, The Philosophy of Freedom, How to Know Higher Worlds, Christianity as a Mystical Fact,* and *Occult Science.*

ABOUT THE AUTHOR, DR. DOUGLAS GABRIEL

Dr. Gabriel is a retired superintendent of schools and professor of education who has worked with schools and organizations throughout the world. He has authored many books ranging from teacher training manuals to philosophical/spiritual works on the nature of the divine feminine.

He was a Waldorf class teacher and administrator at the Detroit Waldorf School and taught courses at Mercy College, the University of Detroit, and Wayne State University for decades. He then became the Headmaster of a Waldorf School in Hawaii and taught at the University of Hawaii, Hilo. He was a leader in the development of charter schools in Michigan and helped found the first Waldorf School in the Detroit Public School system and the first charter Waldorf School in Michigan.

Gabriel received his first degree in religious formation at the same time as an associate degree in computer science in 1972. This odd mixture of technology and religion continued throughout his life. He was drafted into and served in the Army Security Agency (NSA) where he was a cryptologist and systems analyst in signal intelligence, earning him a degree in signal broadcasting. After military service, he entered the Catholic Church again as a Trappist monk and later as a Jesuit priest where he earned PhD's in philosophy and comparative religion, and a Doctor of Divinity. He came to Detroit and earned a BA in anthroposophical studies and history and a MA in school administration. Gabriel left the priesthood and became a

Waldorf class teacher and administrator in Detroit and later in Hilo, Hawaii.

Douglas has been a sought-after lecturer and consultant to schools and businesses throughout the world and in 1982 he founded the Waldorf Educational Foundation that provides funding for the publication of educational books. He has raised a great deal of money for Waldorf schools and institutions that continue to develop the teachings of Dr. Rudolf Steiner. Douglas is now retired but continues to write a variety of books including a novel and a science fiction thriller. He has four children, who keep him busy and active and a wife who is always striving towards the spirit through creating an "art of life." She is the author of the Gospel of Sophia trilogy.

The Gabriels' articles, blogs, and videos can currently be found at:

OurSpirit.com
Neoanthroposphy.com
GospelofSophia.com
EternalCurriculum.com

TRANSLATOR'S NOTE

The Rudolf Steiner quotes in this book can be found, in most cases, in their full-length and in context, through the Rudolf Steiner Archives by an Internet search of the references provided. We present the quoted selections of Steiner from a free rendered translation of the original while utilizing comparisons of numerous German to English translations that are available from a variety of publishers and other sources. In some cases, the quoted selections may be condensed and partially summarized using the same, or similar in meaning, words found in the original. Brackets are used to insert [from the author] clarifying details or anthroposophical nomenclature and spiritual scientific terms.

We chose to use GA (Gesamtausgabe – collected edition) numbers to reference Steiner's works instead of CW (Collected Works), which is often used in English editions. Some books in the series, *From the Works of Rudolf Steiner*, have consciously chosen to use a predominance of Steiner quotes to drive the presentation of the themes rather than personal remarks and commentary.

We feel that Steiner's descriptions should not be truncated but need to be translated into an easily read format for the English-speaking reader, especially for those new to Anthroposophy. We recommend that serious aspirants read the entire lecture, or chapter, from which the Steiner quotation was taken, because nothing can replace Steiner's original words or the mood in which they were delivered. The style of speaking and writing has changed dramatically over the last century and needs updating in style and presentation to translate into a useful tool for spiritual study in modern times. The series, *From the Works of Rudolf Steiner* intends to present numerous "study guides" for the beginning aspirant, and the initiate, in a format that helps support the spiritual scientific research of the reader.

Made in the USA
Middletown, DE
16 November 2024

64699481R00073